THE ISLAND ESCAPE

Getaway Bay, Book 5

ELANA JOHNSON

ISBN-13: 978-1-63876-007-8

Chapter One

Riley Randall leaned her head back as the plane touched down on the island of Getaway Bay. She loved visiting her family. She did. Honestly. But it had been a little bit much with all sixteen of them there, celebrating her parents fiftieth wedding anniversary.

With her four older siblings, her parents, and her six nieces and nephews, Riley had enjoyed a great week on Oahu. She really had.

But she was very happy to be home, in Getaway Bay, where she could eat whatever cereal she wanted in her little bungalow, sleep past six a.m., and have a moment—or two—of silence when she needed it.

She'd definitely felt left out this week, but she knew it wasn't her siblings' fault. They all had a spouse, and she didn't. It was natural to pair up that way, but she'd often been left to herself to find someone to paddle board with, or someone to sit by at dinner, or someone to go with her up to the bathrooms from the beach.

Yes, she was definitely very happy to be home.

The seatbelt sign on the airplane turned off, and a flurry of activity started. She sat near the back of the plane, but she stood up anyway. Because of her petite frame, the top of her head barely touched the underside of the overhead compartment.

It seemed to take forever for the crowd to inch forward, get their bags down, collect their cell phones. Riley normally wasn't impatient, but she needed to go to the bathroom, and she was simply peopled out.

When it was finally her turn, the people on her row moved into the aisle. "Yours is the pink one, right?" the man beside her said, and Riley nodded.

"Yes, thank you."

He got her luggage down for her, and she followed him off the plane. How the flight attendants could still be smiling boggled her mind, and yet she smiled at them as she got off too. So it could be done.

After all, she worked in an industry that required an endless supply of smiles, even when there was nothing to smile about.

Riley sure had enjoyed her time away from Your Tidal Forever. The stress of making sure every appointment got scheduled correctly, with the right person, at the right time. Her boss was somewhat overbearing, but Riley had learned to love Hope. She loved all the people she'd worked with, even if some of them had gone on to get their own happily-ever-after too.

She just wanted one of her own. *And you'll get it*, she told herself as the line in front of her stalled again just after she'd stepped off the plane. She sighed and looked down, her eye catching on something shiny on the jetway.

It was a watch, and she bent to pick it up. "Is this yours?" she asked the man in front of her. He turned and looked at it, shook his head, and moved when the line did.

Concerned, but unsure about what to do with the watch, Riley followed him. No one grabbed onto her arm or demanded she give them the watch. She slipped it into her purse, intending to find out whose it was and return it—right after she took a good, long nap.

LATER THAT EVENING, RILEY HAD SLEPT, UNPACKED HER bag, and put a load of laundry in the washing machine before she remembered the watch. She retrieved it from her purse and attempted to turn it on, but it wouldn't power up.

She examined the charging plug, and she didn't have anything that would fit it. But she knew who did—Shannon Bell, a co-worker at Your Tidal Forever. Riley had seen Shannon wear a watch similar to this one before, albeit in a shade of rosy pink and not this masculine black.

She pulled out her phone and tapped a message to Shannon. *Can you charge this watch?* She snapped a picture of the item and sent it along to Shannon.

Where did you get that?

I found it on the plane, Riley said, though that wasn't technically true. *If I can power it up, I might be able to see who it belongs to.*

I'll bring my charger to work tomorrow.

Work tomorrow.

Riley was tired just thinking about it.

But off to work she went the next day, as it was Monday, and she'd spent the last seven days on vacation. She didn't think it was fair that vacation drained her so much, but she didn't really have anyone to complain to about it.

"And that's not even true," she muttered to herself. After work today, she'd stop by the pet paradise and pick up her two cats, who had been boarded there while she celebrated the beginnings of her family.

So she could definitely complain to Marbles and Sunshine, detail everything for them about the trip, what her sister had said, and the secrets her brother had told her about their other brother.

She smiled just thinking of all of them, and she was glad she still loved them, even after spending so much time with them in such close proximity.

Riley always arrived before almost anyone else at the

wedding planning business. She loved her job, and she was very good at it. Her desk felt like it wasn't quite hers, and she took a half an hour while the rest of the consultants came in to get everything back where it should be.

Shannon finally arrived, her handsome husband continuing down the sidewalk to the building where he worked. Jeremiah was a doctor, and he and Shannon were a perfect fit for one another.

"I brought the charger," Shannon said. "And it's so good to see you." She came around the desk and hugged Riley, and Riley let the feelings of love move through her. See, she didn't need a man. She had girlfriends.

In her heart of hearts, though, Riley knew it wasn't the same. "Thank you. What have I missed?"

"Oh my—holy cow." Shannon covered her mouth. "So much has happened. Charlotte announced that she and Dawson are adopting a baby."

Riley stalled in her movement to plug in the watch. "You're kidding."

"I am really not." Shannon looked like she'd swallowed stars and they now shone in her eyes. "It was very exciting. Hope brought in cake and then she cried through the whole thing."

"Oh, that's too bad." Riley's spirits deflated. Hope and her husband Aiden had been trying to have kids for a while, and it just wasn't working out.

Shannon's phone rang, and she said, "We have to lunch today and get caught up," before walking a few steps and answering the call.

Riley finished plugging in the watch, enjoying the little chimes it made as it powered on. Now, she'd just figure out who this device belonged to, and she'd have done her good deed for the day.

Four days later, Riley slipped into the bathroom to check her hair. She was meeting one Evan Garfield today to return the watch she'd found on the jetway. He'd confirmed a few things on the watch, so Riley was sure it was him, plus it had been his email address she'd sent the message to about finding the watch.

He'd apparently been on the island for a concert, and he was still in town. "So you don't need to check your hair," she muttered to her reflection. "He's a tourist, Riley. You don't date tourists."

But she was seriously considering it, as it seemed like she'd been through all the eligible bachelors on the island that were permanent residents.

Still, some measure of hope bounced around in her chest as she exited the bathroom, grabbed the watch from her desk drawer, and headed out. She and Evan were meeting at Roasted on the other side of East Bay, and she opted to walk though the September sun would melt her makeup off her face after about five minutes.

She showed up early and scanned the place for someone who looked like an Evan. Almost scoffing at herself—because what did an Evan even look like?—she moved over to the counter and ordered a latte with cream.

Hardly anyone actually came inside Roasted, choosing instead to use their drive-through window, so she hadn't thought to give the guy her physical description. It wasn't like they were going on a blind date. She shook her head at her romantic ideas about passing off a lost item.

The bell on the door rang, and three men entered. They all wore beanies, which Riley found odd, and sunglasses, which fit the Hawaiian atmosphere. She watched them approach the counter, wondering if one of them could be Evan.

They all wore jeans and some version of a Georgia Panic T-shirt, which Riley found odd. Something jiggled in the back of her brain about the band, but she couldn't put her finger on what. Then the barista set her latte down in front of her and turned to the men.

Distracted by the delicious coffee, Riley twisted away from them and sipped her hot caffeine. The stool next to her scraped, and a man said, "Is this seat taken?"

"It is by you," Riley said with a smile in his general direction. The other two men stayed down by the register, and neither looked in her direction.

"You know that has a plastic straw in it, right?" He nodded to her drink.

Riley simply lifted the little red straw to her lips and sucked on her latte. The liquid was much too hot to take much into her mouth, but she did it anyway, never removing her eyes from the man next to her.

He had a sexy scruff going on, and if he'd take off those sunglasses, Riley would bet money she'd find a beautiful pair of dark eyes beneath those bushy brows. His hair was dark poking out of the beanie, with that beard to match.

"I'll tie it in a knot before I throw it away," she said.

"That doesn't always work." He plucked a napkin from the dispenser on the counter. "A lot of sea animals die from the plastic in the oceans."

Riley had read all about it. "I'm surprised someone like you knows that," she said, teasing him and hoping he could hear it. She'd never seen him or the men with him around the island, and she was probably flirting with a tourist.

But these guys didn't seem like tourists. No board shorts. No flip flops. No long, blond hair. T-shirts and jeans really stood out on the island, and she wondered who they were and what they were doing in Getaway Bay.

"Someone like me?" he asked.

"Yeah," she said. "Someone so handsome and tall and obviously into the same coffee as me." She nodded toward the cup as the barista set down another latte—with a little red, plastic straw in it.

The man chuckled, and Riley really wanted to get his name and number. She glanced toward the door, her thoughts about Evan somewhere way below this guy. She almost didn't want him to show up.

"And your friends sat over there," she said, pointing with that straw. "Did you guys have some sort of bro code or something?"

The man laughed again, his version of saying yes.

"Are you new on the island?" she asked.

"What gave it away?" he asked.

"The lack of swimming gear," she said. "The jeans. The beanie in September. I don't know. I just have a way of knowing."

"Do you live here?"

"Yep."

"Raised here?"

"No, I grew up on Oahu, but I've lived in Getaway Bay for oh, let's see. At least a decade now." She reminded herself she was thirty-five years old now. So she'd been on the island for twelve years, not just ten. She didn't correct herself though. Two years didn't make a difference to this guy.

But two years made a lot of difference to Riley.

"So, you locals regularly get coffee in the middle of the day, when it's super hot outside?" he asked.

"Oh, honey," she said, playfully putting one of her immaculately manicured hands on his arm. "It's not super hot right now. Maybe in July." She twittered out a laugh she hoped would earn her his number and looked at him.

"So why are you here?" he asked, scanning her clothes. "Are you drinking coffee for lunch?"

"Today I am," she said, taking another sip.

"Do you work around here?"

"Other side of the bay," she said. "A wedding planning place."

He nodded as if he knew the spot, but Riley knew he didn't. She couldn't help herself, though. Maybe she just wanted to prove she still had some game when it came to flirting with gorgeous men.

"What does a guy have to do to get your number?" he asked.

"Give me your phone." She held out her palm, victory only breaths away. "My name's Riley, by the way."

He handed her his phone, and she started tapping on it to get to his contacts and put herself in them. She paused, realizing he hadn't given her his name.

"Riley Randall?" he asked.

"Yeah." An alarm sounded in her head as she cocked it. "Who are you?"

"I'm Evan Garfield. I think you have my watch."

Chapter Two

Evan could not believe the gorgeous brunette he'd just picked up in the coffee shop also had his watch. Those gorgeous green eyes rounded, and she dissolved into giggles. "Oh, wow. Let me get it for you."

She started digging in her purse, and Evan decided he could let her use of plastic straws slide if she'd laugh for him again. "Here it is." She pulled out the watch, said, "Oops," and immediately dropped it.

A sharp crack sounded as the face of it met the concrete floor in the coffee shop, and Riley was off her barstool in a moment. "Oh, my goodness. I'm so sorry. I can't believe this." She picked up the watch, which sure enough, was now broken. She looked at him, pure panic in her eyes now. "I've taken such good care of it for four days."

Evan absolutely did not care about the watch. In fact, he'd already replaced it, as it had been missing for over a week now. "It's fine," he said, covering her fingers with his. An electric spark flew up his arm, and he slowly dragged his hand back, taking the broken watch with him. "No big deal."

"It is a big deal," she said. "Let me replace it for you."

"Sit down," he said, indicating her barstool again. "Honestly, Riley, I don't care about the watch." He lifted his left wrist, where an identical one sat. "See?"

She blinked rapidly again. "You already have another one?"

"That's right." He didn't want to tell her too much right now, as most people saw him differently once they knew who he really was. In fact, with his clothes and his brother's tees, he was surprised she hadn't put all the pieces together yet. If there were other people in this shop, he'd probably have been recognized by now.

Riley's barstool scraped and his phone hit the countertop at the same time. "Excuse me," she said, and before Evan could even move, she was out the door of the coffee shop.

"Wow," Carl said, also watching the door close behind Riley. "She can run fast." His youngest brother could sometimes point out the obvious, which only added to Evan's irritation.

"What just happened?" Evan picked up his phone, and thankfully, the screen wasn't broken. Riley also hadn't put in her number. Desperation pulled through him, and he frowned as he looked at the door again.

"She didn't even finish her latte," Brett said as he came over. The middle brother, he almost always tried to get Evan and Carl to get along. "What did you say to her?"

"Nothing, I—" He shook his head. Her reaction was why he'd struck out with women more often than not. "Maybe she recognized me."

"Why would that make her run?" Carl asked. "Besides the fact that you haven't shaved in forever."

Evan rolled his eyes as he stood up. "Can I get this to go?" he asked the barista.

She nodded and took his drink. When she handed it back to him in a paper cup, she said, "I saw your concert the other night. You guys are great."

"Thanks," Evan said, his easy-going, rockstar smile coming out. He couldn't help it. Brett, as the band's public relations front person, had programmed Southern kindness and cordiality into him. Into all the band members of Georgia Panic. Evan just happened to be the front guy, the one whose name everyone knew, the one on the covers of magazines, the one getting stupid "awards" like Sexiest Man Alive.

Okay, maybe that last one was pretty cool.

Hadn't helped him get a woman worth keeping, though.

"Did you get her number?" Carl asked.

"No," Evan said.

"But you got the watch back," he pointed out.

"I don't care about the watch." Evan tossed it in the

trashcan on the way out, trying to remember where she'd said she worked. "It's broken now anyway. I was just going to give it to DJ." His bass guitarist would be disappointed, but it wasn't like he couldn't afford his own smart watch.

Evan paused in the shade and pushed up his glasses. "Did either of you see which way she went?"

"You really liked her?" Carl asked.

"Yeah," Evan said. "She was beautiful, and she flirted with me, and I was seconds away from getting her number." He looked at his phone again, but the digits didn't appear there. He wasn't sure what about Riley had him all worked up, but there was something. A huge spark when she touched his arm. An intense attraction between them. He had to see her again.

"So you have her email," Brett said, nudging him to get moving again. Neither of his brothers had wanted to come to the coffee shop on the beach. But Evan rarely went anywhere on his own, and he was going no matter what anyone said. So they'd come along too. "We have a meet-and-greet at City Hall in an hour. You'll email her tonight, after the show."

"All right," Evan drawled, ready to be done with this tour. Thankfully, Getaway Bay was their last stop, and tonight would be their last show.

Then he wanted some of those board shorts Riley had mentioned. He wanted to ditch the street clothes and the beanies and the oversized sunglasses and lay on the beach. He needed to *relax*.

He'd earned a beach vacation, and he was going to take it—right after tonight's concert. And right after he emailed Riley and figured out a way to see her again.

THREE DAYS. THREE AGONIZINGLY LONG DAYS, AND RILEY had not answered his email. He'd been lying on the beach. Tanning. Wearing those board shorts she'd mentioned and nothing else. But he had not been relaxing. He couldn't, not without knowing that she'd gotten his message.

"Why would she be avoiding me?" he asked, looking over at DJ.

"This again?" the man asked, turning away from his girlfriend.

"You need to figure out where she works," Lisa said. "I don't get how you can't remember. You talked to her for like, three minutes, and she told you very little."

"Exactly," Evan said, very near to snapping. "She told me very little."

"She said she worked on the other side of the bay," DJ said, wiping his hand over his shaved head. "What did she do?"

Evan closed his eyes and pictured Riley. Petite brunette, with long hair and long eyelashes. So perfectly perched on that barstool, swirling that plastic straw in her coffee. He was no stranger to lattes, and he'd known she was drinking one without having to get too close. So he'd ordered one too.

"Wedding planning," he said, feeling the ghost of her fingers on his arm.

"Give me a sec," Lisa said, her fingers already tapping on her phone. "There are a couple of wedding planning places on the island."

"Send 'im a list," DJ said. "And maybe he'll stop obsessing over this woman."

Evan wanted to argue. Say he wasn't obsessed. But he kind of was. He'd started a few songs about Riley, each one dying a few lyrics in. He'd come back to them, sure. He knew how his songwriting approach went by now.

His phone chimed, and he almost dove for it before realizing it was probably Lisa with the list of places. Riley hadn't said which one, and she hadn't used a work email. They'd corresponded several times about the watch, so he knew she checked her email on a regular basis.

So she'd chosen not to respond to him. A frown pulled at his eyebrows again, and he wondered if he should just let this woman go. She obviously wasn't interested in him.

Then the roar of fireworks would fill his veins, and he knew he had to at least try. So he dialed the top name on the list and said, "Yes, hello. I'm looking for Riley Randall…she doesn't? Okay, thanks." He hung up, his heart pounding in his chest.

He got this same rush while standing up on the stage

before a show, when all the lights were off, and the drums were beating, beating, beating.

No one knew he was there yet, but he knew. In those few moments, he breathed, and he reminded himself how grateful he was to be able to do what he did. Sing, and song-write, and entertain. He loved every minute of it.

Then the lights would come on, and the crowd would scream, and Evan could feed off that energy. Calling around, looking for Riley, felt like that.

"This has to be it," he said as he finally got to the bottom of the list. The phone rang, and his heart swooped to the bottom of his stomach. What would he do if she wasn't at this wedding planning place either?

"Your Tidal Forever," a woman chirped, and the voice struck a chord in Evan's brain.

"Yes, hi," he said, changing tactics quickly. "I'm looking for the *gorgeous* brunette who ran away from me at the coffee shop. Do you happen to know when she takes her lunch?"

On the other end of the line, Riley sucked in a breath and said, "Hold, please." A click immediately followed, and joy filled Evan from top to bottom.

He laughed, stood up, and said, "I'm going to Your Tidal Forever."

"Tell Carl," DJ yelled after him, but Evan didn't even know where Carl was at the moment, and he could certainly go off on his own. He was forty-two years old, for crying out loud.

Chapter Three

"What do you mean you put him on hold?" Charlotte asked. "That was him?"

Panic built inside Riley's chest. "He found me."

"He must be really interested." Charlotte smiled and shook her head, clearly trying to understand why Riley had a death grip on the phone and wouldn't pick it up. Riley had no explanation for her. She didn't understand anything right now.

She knew Evan Garfield could most certainly not be interested in her. He was the lead singer for Georgia Panic, a world-famous band that had just finished their multi-billion dollar tour right here in Getaway Bay.

She'd berated herself for three days that she hadn't recognized him. Had to be the beanie, the sneak.

And he'd emailed her, asking for her number and to go out for another latte. She'd ignored him, hoping that would be that.

And now he was on hold.

"He knows where I work now." She groaned, because she didn't need the tall, handsome rockstar to walk through the door. Panicking fully now, she cut a glance toward the door. No one was there.

"I'll talk to him," Charlotte said, and before Riley could move, her friend had picked up the phone. "Yes, hello, this is Charlotte Dane. How may I help you?" A few seconds passed. "Hello?"

Riley looked at her, desperate for news. "What? What's he saying?"

Charlotte hung up the phone, and Riley almost started crying. She was all over the place right now, wanting to talk to Evan and not wanting to. "He's not there. The line was dead."

Dead.

Like Riley's nerves these last few days.

But a rockstar?

A multi-platinum lead singer?

The sexiest man alive?

No, no, no. He was *not* interested in *her*.

"Maybe I dodged a bullet," she said as Charlotte rounded the front desk and headed for her office. She looked down at her computer, at a calendar she'd been organizing before Evan's call had come in.

"Uh, Riley?"

"Yeah?" She looked up again to find Charlotte frozen, facing the front door.

The bell on it chimed a moment later, and none other than the gorgeous Evan Garfield walked in. Alone. Wearing only board shorts.

Riley stared at his beautiful, tan skin, those muscles that bumped their way up his chest, finally looking into those eyes for the very first time.

And she was so right. They were dark, and dreamy, and absolutely dangerous to her health.

"I found you," he said easily, as if he hadn't stolen the last three nights of good sleep from her. "Why didn't you answer my email?"

Riley blinked, kicking herself into action. "You emailed?"

He chuckled, which so wasn't fair. "You're not a good liar."

No, she wasn't, and she had no idea what to say next.

"When is your lunch?" he asked, repeating his question from the phone call.

"Right now," Charlotte said before Riley could make a peep. "She was *just* saying how she wanted a big salad from Pepe's."

"Charlotte," Riley growled.

"Great," Evan said as if Riley hadn't spoken. "I haven't eaten there yet, but our drummer says it's fantastic."

Our drummer.

So he wasn't trying to hide who he was anymore. Curiosity nagged at Riley, and she wondered why he'd put on the costume to meet her at the coffee shop a few days ago. Her mother had always told her that curiosity killed the cat, but today, it was going to buy her lunch.

"Fine," she said, pouring her frustration into her voice. "You can buy me a salad at Pepe's." She left her purse secured in her bottom drawer and just grabbed her phone. She glared at Charlotte as she passed, but Charlotte gave her a double thumbs-up.

How embarrassing.

Riley avoided looking directly at Evan as she passed, though she felt the weight of his smile. She felt as hot as the sun as she went outside ahead of him, who didn't seem to notice or care about the tension in the air. But it choked her, and she didn't know how to get rid of it.

A breeze blew off the bay, and she paused for a moment, trying to get a decent breath.

"She seems nice," Evan said, sidling up beside her. "How long have you known her?"

"A while," Riley said, as she didn't normally talk about her friends while flirting with a man. It seemed surreal that she'd attracted this man's attention at the coffee shop. *There was no one else there*, she told herself, just as she'd been doing for the past few days.

"How'd you get here so fast?" she asked, finally allowing herself to look at him. Oh, that was a mistake, because her stomach took a dive, and her heartbeat started sprinting, and everything female in her wanted to give him her phone number. Then they could have this lunch together, and text all afternoon as they made plans for dinner.

Without the beanie, she could see his head full of dark brown hair. The beach breeze played with it, and Riley was jealous of a wind for the first time in her life. Evan slid a pair of sunglasses over his eyes, but she'd seen the depth of them. No wonder he'd been voted Sexiest Man Alive. Those eyes could devour a woman in less time than it took to inhale.

"I was just sitting down the beach a bit," he said, pointing north. "With a couple of friends. You want to meet them?"

She let her gaze drip down his body and back to his face. "You'll need a shirt for Pepe's."

A grin burst onto his face. "Ah, so there's the woman I met at the coffee shop." He leaned closer, though the hot concrete had to be burning his feet. "I've been waiting for you to email me back, you know."

Riley started walking, because then the conversation would flow better. She'd be able to look somewhere besides right at him, and maybe the sky would swallow some of her insecurity. "I wasn't going to email you back," she said.

"Why not?" Evan's hand brushed hers, and Riley really wanted to grab onto his fingers. She didn't, her throat sticky now.

"Because," she said. "I have a strict no-dating-tourists rule for myself."

"I'm not a tourist," he said.

She started laughing, but it wasn't the flirtatious kind that told a man she wanted him to ask her for her number. More maniacal. Riley felt wildly out of control, and that wasn't a good thing. It meant she'd say whatever came to her mind, and she always regretted doing so afterward.

"You don't live here," she said.

"Well, that's true."

"In fact, you maintain residences in Sutherland Heights, Grand Cayman, and California." She looked at him, her eyebrows cocked.

"Maybe I'll maintain one in Getaway Bay," he said easily, meeting her gaze. "It's really beautiful here." He paused, touching her arm to get her to stop too.

She froze, because the zinging of electrons up her arm required all of her thought.

"*You're* really beautiful," he said. "And I feel like I've missed out on three days of getting to know you. Three days of fun. Three days of big salads and laughing on the beach and texting all night long."

Riley blinked at him, sure she'd started hallucinating. Men didn't talk like this. Did they?

Evan's not just any man, she told herself. He was a freaking rock icon. Every woman in the world would probably give a kidney to meet him, and she'd held his phone for a few seconds, about to put her number in it.

No wonder she hadn't emailed him back. He wasn't real. She'd legit gone crazy.

"Evan," someone called, and relief rushed through Riley. His entourage would sweep him away from her, and she wouldn't have to come up with a response to the most perfect words on the planet.

She faded a step or two behind him as he gave his attention to a tattooed man walking toward them, sand flying around his feet as he walked. DJ Brickey, the bass player. He was almost as famous as Evan Garfield, swoon-worthy, sexy, mysterious lead singer of Georgia Panic. A rail-thin woman came with DJ, and they both looked at Riley and smiled.

"Oh, you found her," DJ said. "Hey there. I'm DJ Brickey." He extended his hand for her to shake, which she managed to do. "My partner, Lisa."

"So great to meet you," Lisa said, shaking her hand too. "Evan's been talking—"

"Thanks, Lisa," Evan said loudly. "And I did find her. We were just coming to meet you and let you know we're going to Pepe's for lunch." He did not invite them to come with him.

"Your brother isn't going to be happy about that."

"Oh, Carl will be fine," Evan said dismissively. "I'm on *vacation*, and I don't need a babysitter." He glanced at Riley, and she couldn't be quite sure, but it certainly looked like a flush had entered his face.

"Why won't Carl be happy about Pepe's?" Riley asked.

Everyone stared at her for two breaths, and then DJ started laughing. "I see why you like her." He threaded his fingers through Lisa's, and they turned back toward a smattering of towels on the sand. DJ stooped to pick up a Frisbee, and he jogged toward the shoreline where a few other men stood.

"So those are some of my friends," Evan said, still watching them. He reached over and tentatively slipped his fingers through Riley's. "Carl won't like me going off on my own. My brother's a little overprotective of me, though I'm the oldest."

Riley really liked the way his hand felt in hers. She looked at their fingers and then up to his face. "You're the oldest? I'm the youngest."

"Of how many?" he asked, gently tugging on her hand to get her moving again.

"Five," she said. "Two older brothers and two older sisters."

"Are you close with them?" he asked.

Riley had easy access to a lot of things about Evan. How old he was. His middle name. Where he'd grown up. His past relationships. It was all right there on the Internet, and she'd read some of it in pure disbelief that he'd sat down beside her at the coffee shop and flirted with her.

"Yes," she said, bringing herself back to this moment. She vowed she wouldn't look up anything else about him. That way, she could get to know him the way she would any other man. "I just got back from a week-long anniversary party for my parents. It was their fiftieth."

"Oh, wow," Evan said, chuckling. "Good for them."

"Yeah, it was a little crazy," Riley said, starting to relax. Strolling down the boardwalk, hand-in-hand with a gorgeous man, was pretty much what she dreamed about at night. "But I do love them."

"I have the two brothers," he said. "They're part of the management team for the band. So I spend every day with them."

Riley glanced at him again, finding this personal side of him...refreshing. "You sound...neutral about that?"

"Neutral? I guess." He shrugged. "Carl and I argue a lot. Brett tries to make us get along."

"I'm kind of the black sheep in my family," she said.

"In what way?"

"Well, everyone but me is married," she said. "So they all have someone. I have six nieces and nephews, and my sister is pregnant, so they'll all have children soon." She watched the waves roll in for a few seconds. "So I don't quite fit."

"I understand that," he said. "I don't quite fit anywhere I go."

"That's because you're a famous rockstar and easily recognizable." She bumped him with her shoulder, realizing he'd never gotten that shirt.

He chuckled and ducked his head. "You didn't recognize me at the coffee shop."

"The beanie really threw me off," she teased. "And now this shirtless look is tripping me out." She stared at his chest, memorizing the lines of a tattoo he had running across his right shoulder, almost kissing his collarbone.

She cleared her throat at the same time he pulled his hand away. "Be right back." He took a couple of steps back the way they'd come. "Wait." He turned toward her again. "Don't disappear again, okay?"

"You know where I work now," she said. "I can't disappear for long."

He grinned and jogged toward the towels, where a couple more people had gathered—including the two from the coffee shop. His brothers. She'd read that they were the trio of intellect behind the band, and Brett wrote music and songs while Carl managed the band. He booked gigs, and managed personalities and schedules, and probably did a lot of what Riley did for Your Tidal Forever.

They both looked toward her as Evan pulled a T-shirt over his head, covering all those delicious muscles and all that tan skin.

All three of them came toward her, and Riley really wanted to run again. The storm on Evan's face broadcasted his displeasure, but he hadn't told his brothers no.

"Riley," he said as he got closer. "This is my brother, Carl." He indicated the man directly next to him. "And Brett."

"So great to meet you properly," Brett said, oozing Southern charm and kindness. Their mother had taught them well, that was for sure.

"Thank you," Riley said. She'd worked with a lot of

high-profile brides—and their mothers—in stressful situations. She could meet the Garfield brothers. "You too." She shook his hand and then Carl's, who didn't say anything.

"So we're going to lunch," Evan said, stepping in front of them. "Riley has to be back to work soon, so I won't be gone long."

"You have your phone?" Carl asked.

"Yes, Mother," Evan said with a laugh, nudging Riley to turn around. They walked away, but Riley could plainly feel the weight of four eyes on her back.

"Sorry about that," Evan said. "Sometimes they forget I'm forty-two and not four."

"You don't go off on your own very often," she said, pieces clicking together. "That was why you brought them to the coffee shop."

"Oh, Carl was convinced you were some crazed fan, claiming to have my watch." Evan claimed her hand again, and Riley could get used to her rockstar boyfriend coming to get her for lunch each day.

"Maybe I am," she said.

"Yeah, I don't think so." Evan leaned closer, the heat from his body setting Riley's cells on fire. "You didn't even know who I was. It was very refreshing."

"And you don't get many people who don't know who you are," she said, everything becoming clearer now. If she had fallen all over him, he wouldn't have given her the time of day. Literally. He'd have taken his watch back and gotten the heck out of the coffee shop with his brother bodyguards.

She should pull her hand away, claim she wasn't hungry, and hurry back to her desk. She almost did, but Evan kneaded her closer and said, "You're not running away from me again, Riley Randall."

Chapter Four

Evan could sense Riley's tension as it skyrocketed, and he'd said something she didn't like.

"I don't want to go out with you," she said, but there was no power behind the words.

"Why not?"

"You don't live here," she said. "And I have a—"

"Policy," they said together. "I heard," he added. "And this isn't about your policy." He kept walking, every step away from her office a victory. "You think I only liked you because you didn't know who I was."

"Or you're delusional," she said. "Neither is playing in your favor."

He smiled, because she was witty and quick, and he liked that. "I'm not delusional," he said. "I know what I like, and you…I liked you."

"Yeah, I heard DJ say that," she said. "What have you been saying about me?

"Honestly?"

She laughed again, not quite getting the humor in the sound. He didn't really like that, but he supposed she needed some time to warm up to the idea of dating him. He knew he was a lot to handle. His lifestyle. His personality. He'd been told more than once that he was intense, both on stage and in his private life.

He didn't know how else to be. He wanted to experience everything in life, savor each day, breathe through each moment.

"You better be honest with me," Riley said. "Otherwise, I should take you back to your brothers right now."

"Yeah, pass," he said. "Okay, so honestly. I've been a little…obsessive the last couple of days trying to figure out why you wouldn't respond to my email. It was Lisa who searched for a list of wedding planning places and told me to call. And she only did it so I'd shut up about you."

"This is unbelievable," Riley said.

"It's the honest truth." Evan watched a bird fly overhead. "DJ said I was moody. Pete texts me every morning to find out if you've contacted me yet. He went back to the states for his break. Carl rolls his eyes when I check my phone and frown." He laughed, because he supposed his behavior the past few days had been a little ridiculous. "But hey, I found you, and I won't have to be that moody Evan anymore."

"What if I say I don't want to go out with you?"

"Is that what you want to say?" he asked, his pulse

ricocheting around inside his chest. What would he do if she said yeah, she didn't want to see him again?

"I'm just asking what if," she said.

"I don't do what if's," he said. "I just deal with stuff as it actually happens." He grinned at her as if he was oh-so-wise.

"This is a little surreal for me," she said. "I mean, you're a rockstar. You've been on the cover of *People*." She shook her head, and Evan almost wished none of those things were true. That they'd never happened.

"I'm just a guy," he said. "A guy who really liked you in the coffee shop. A guy you were going to give your number to before you knew who I was. Why can't I just be that guy?"

"Because, Evan." She paused and looked up at him. "You're not *just that guy*, and you know it."

"I like it when you say my name."

"And no guy just says whatever he's thinking," she said. "That's weird." She stepped past him, removing her hand from his, and he thought she'd walked out of his life again. Then he realized they'd somehow arrived at Pepe's, and she'd gone inside.

A smile started to fill his soul. She hadn't run away. And he needed to stop saying whatever came to mind. And buy a house on this island, stat.

He followed her inside and joined her in line. "I won't say whatever's on my mind," he said. "I'm not totally weird."

"Everyone is staring at you," she said. "So you're definitely weird."

"Maybe they're staring at you." He refused to look around at the people in the restaurant, choosing instead to study the menu.

"Maybe we should get this food to go."

"Nope," Evan said, sliding his hand along Riley's lower back and letting it rest on her hip. She didn't flinch or move away from him. In fact, she leaned into him, and Evan couldn't even read the menu at that point. She smelled amazing, like peaches and oranges and other tropical fruits, and she fit right in his arms.

"First rule for us," he said. "We don't run from hard things."

"We have to have rules?" she asked, inching forward.

"Well, Carl likes rules, and I'll admit they make some things easier."

"How about rule two, then?" Riley asked, gently pushing his hand off her hip. "You don't crowd me in line."

"As long as you don't run," he said, chuckling. "I can handle that."

Riley cut him a look out of the corner of her eye, and she probably meant it to be a glare. But those green eyes held too much sparkle, and a rush moved through Evan the way waves crashed against the shore.

"I just need to say one more thing on my mind," he said.

"Oh, boy." Riley rolled her eyes playfully. "Go on, then. And you better be ready to order."

"You order for me," he said. "Because all I can think about is if I'm going to walk away from this restaurant with your number in my phone."

She giggled, and Evan had his answer. He still wanted to hear her say it though. She tucked her hair behind her ear and stepped up to the cashier to order. He just went with her, watching her as she ordered her big salad and then a platter of pork nachos for him.

Perfect.

She was *perfect*, and Evan couldn't believe she'd found his watch and tracked him down. Riley handed him a cup and said, "Chances are, you're going to get my number."

"Oh, I need a definitive yes or no," he said.

She walked over to the soda machine and said, "All right, then. Yes," in that fun, flirty voice that had been haunting him since he'd met her in the coffee shop. And with that single word, he knew his vacation was about to get a lot more interesting.

By the time Evan left the restaurant, he not only had Riley's number, but a date with her that night. She'd claimed she was going to be "so late" and "in real trouble" when she got back to the office, and she couldn't see him again until eight o'clock that evening.

He sighed as he sank onto the blanket on the beach, where his family and friends hadn't moved in the two hours he'd been gone. Someone—probably Brett—had put up a huge umbrella for shade, and Evan stripped his shirt off as he scanned the beach for someone he knew.

No one had bothered him at Pepe's, which was an amazing Mexican restaurant just down the boardwalk and across the street. It had quieted after they'd gotten their food, and Riley had allowed him to sit with his back to the crowd. He was used to getting stared at, though he still didn't like it. Used to giving autographs, and giving hugs and high-fives, and getting pictures taken.

He'd promised Riley to take her somewhere off the beaten path for their date that night, and a blip of unrest moved through him. He'd been on the island of Getaway Bay for a week now, but he didn't know hardly any paths, beaten or unbeaten.

He called the hotel where he was staying, glad the concierge had given him his direct line. "Hey, Nate," he said when the man answered in his crisp, professional voice—very much like the one Riley had used to answer the phone earlier. "It's Evan Garfield. I'm wondering if you can give me the name of some…private restaurants or places to go tonight."

"Of course," the man said. "For how many people?"

"Two," he said. "I don't want anything too fancy." Riley didn't seem like the type of woman to appreciate it when a man threw his money around, though Evan had plenty of that. "I want slow, summer night. Somewhere where not a lot of crowds hang out."

"Are you willing to drive?"

The thought of Riley cuddled up with him in the back seat of a luxury car increased Evan's internal temperature about fifty degrees. "Sure," he said. "If you can get me a car service. I don't have a vehicle on the island." In fact, Evan hadn't driven for himself much in the past five years. He owned a motorcycle in each of the cities where he had houses, and that usually did just fine for him.

And Riley in a sexy helmet, on the back of a bike, holding onto him….

"I can get you a service, sir," Nate said. "The North Shore is beautiful in the evening. It's got a cool vibe, and there are much less people there. Everyone is…chill."

"Chill sounds great," Evan said.

"Seafood okay?"

"Yep."

"I'll get you a table at Oceanside," Nate said. "Excellent views. Private booths. Access to a beach with sea turtles that only restaurant-goers can visit. It's very low-key."

Evan appreciated that Nate didn't say "romantic," though he'd somehow gotten that clue from Evan anyway. "Sounds amazing."

"What time can I make the reservation?"

"Uh, later," Evan said. "I can't leave until eight."

"I'll make it for nine-fifteen," he said. "It's only about fifty minutes up to the North Shore."

"Thanks, man," Evan said. "You're the best."

"Of course, sir," Nate said, and Evan thought he could definitely hear a smile in the man's voice. He'd be sure to put a wad of cash on the man's desk when he went back to the hotel to shower. They were staying at one of the higher levels at Sweet Breeze, and he had access to their private beach and a pool only guests on that floor could use. But everyone had wanted to try out the East Bay today, and Evan liked that it was a little less crowded on this side.

"How'd it go?" Brett asked, coming out of nowhere and sitting beside Evan.

"So great." He smiled at his more laid-back brother. "I got her number, *and* we're going out tonight."

Brett chuckled as he shook his head. "I'm kind of surprised at this."

"I know, right?" Evan said. "I never do this." And he didn't. He toured the country as Georgia Panic performed, and he wasn't one of those rockstars with women in his room every night. His one and only marriage had taught him so much, though it had fallen apart after only two years.

He hadn't thought about Kitty in a decade, and it had been fifteen years since their relationship had shattered him. He'd been so busy with the band, and music, and everything taking off that he hadn't dated in a long time.

He went out with someone here and there, mostly for show. To an event. An awards show. Something like that. But a real date, where he got to hold a woman's hand and talk to her? Learn about her? Think about kissing her?

Yeah, he hadn't done that in a long, long time.

"What if this thing with Riley becomes serious?" Brett asked.

"Are you Carl?" Evan asked, laughing. Brett joined in with him, but they both sobered pretty quickly.

"I don't know," Evan said. "We're not touring again for a while, and maybe I'll just stay here."

"And what? Fly to LA for band meetings?"

"Sure," Evan said. "Why not?" He looked at his brother, his mind firing through possibilities. "I mean, Hank just videoed in for most of the last two songs while he stayed in Nashville with Melinda." The backup vocalist and keyboardist had become a father while they'd been working on their last album, and he'd caught up fine once he'd made it to LA. "And there are other places to record."

"Sure, sure," Brett said, which meant he was still thinking about things. Evan appreciated that his brother actually did think before he spoke, because Carl would've just told him how ridiculous he was being, and that he couldn't stay in Getaway Bay because of a pretty face.

But Carl hadn't felt the sparks shooting through Evan's whole body when he touched Riley. There was something between them, and Evan wanted to find out if it could grow and morph and bloom into something lasting.

After all, he wasn't getting any younger, and he wouldn't be a rockstar forever. He thought about what Riley had told him about her loud, obnoxious family, and he wanted one of his own.

None of his brothers had significant others, and maybe it was time to stop dragging them all over the world so they had a shot at a more normal life.

Evan wanted it all—he always had. Normalcy at home. Fame on the road. Private time to pluck a guitar and work through troublesome lyrics. Public time to show the world what gifts God had given him.

"I want a family," he said, only realizing he'd said it out loud when Brett said, "Yeah, I hear you, bro. I hear you."

"You do too?"

"I've been thinking it might be time for me to settle down," Brett said with a shrug. "Here comes Carl. Don't say anything to him about this. Please."

"Deal," Evan said as Carl stopped in front of them.

"What's the deal?" he demanded, and Evan just started laughing.

Chapter Five

Riley had to hustle to get caught up from the work she'd missed during her long lunch. The height of the summer weddings had passed, but that only meant that the consultants at Your Tidal Forever had moved on to their holiday season.

"Lisa," she said into the phone, waiting for one of her best friends to respond before continuing.

"Go ahead, Riley," she said, and Riley wished she could sit down with Lisa for just ten minutes and talk about Evan. Charlotte was a good friend, but she was married, and her perspective was different. Lisa would be a better sounding board.

So while she wanted to ask to grab tea that afternoon, she simply said, "I have the Pyne file ready for you, and Gillian called to say she'd be fifteen minutes late."

Lisa sighed into the phone. "That woman is never on time."

"I can call Fiona and see if she can push back fifteen minutes," Riley offered, as Lisa had back-to-back appointments that afternoon.

"If you would, that would be amazing," Lisa said. "And I heard something about a rockstar stopping by for you earlier…bring me the Pyne file, would you?"

Riley almost squealed, but she simply said, "I'll be right there," and hung up. She prepared a lot of files for the consultants at Your Tidal Forever. They had a ton of meetings, not only with brides, their mothers, and their grooms, but with vendors as well.

Riley kept track of all the appointments—at least those the consultants remembered to put into the calendar—the receipts, the surveys every bride filled out, the timeline of when everything needed to be booked, ordered, or sampled. The paperwork was never-ending, but Riley actually liked looking at a stack of papers and organizing them into something manageable and easily referenced.

She picked up the file with the blue stickers PYN on them and headed down the hall. Shannon came her way, walking with a man who did a ton of their announcements. He had his thick binder of specialty papers, and Riley wanted him to stop by her desk so she could leaf through them, stroke the silky papers, and dream about the font she'd use on her own wedding announcements.

"Good afternoon," she said, surprised by her thoughts. Since her dating history hadn't been going great the past several years, some of her dreams about her own wedding had faded. But with the appearance of the gorgeous Evan Garfield in her life, they'd apparently come roaring back.

"Oh, Riley, I need to talk to you for a moment." She glanced at Andrew, whose step barely hitched.

"I'll wait for you at the front desk," he said, and Shannon grinned at him.

She turned to Riley and put her hand on her arm. "Charlotte said you went out with Evan Garfield." Shannon's eyes sparkled as if she were about to get the juiciest secret spilled to her. "And took an extra-long lunch."

"I'm staying late to make up for that," Riley said, her version of saying yes, she'd gone out with a rockstar.

Her.

A rockstar.

She couldn't contain the smile as it spread across her face. Shannon started giggling, and then she said, "I have to tell you not to make a habit of taking a long lunch." She glanced over her shoulder, looking further into the depths of Your Tidal Forever. "Just so I can tell Hope I did. But I know you'll stay on top of your work here."

"I totally will."

"When are you seeing him again?"

"Tonight," Riley said, her muscles tightening with anticipation already. "It's kind of surreal."

"How long is he on the island?" Shannon asked, and that effectively took all the wind out of Riley's sails.

"I don't know," she said. "I have to get this file to Lisa, and then I have three phone calls to make before businesses close." She could file paperwork and make to-do lists for the following day after five p.m.

"Of course, yes." Shannon gave her a quick hug and added, "Text me all the details. I'm so excited for you." She continued down the hall, every piece of her in the perfect place. Shannon had been through a lot too, and Riley knew her friend was excited for her and would want to know all the details. And not just so she could gossip either.

The women at Your Tidal Forever generally got along really great, and they were a good support for one another. Riley had been with the company for eight years, and while she'd undergone some recent personal changes, her job and her friendships within it had always been a constant for her.

She paused in Lisa's doorway and tossed her long, dark hair over her shoulder. "I guess the new look attracted someone."

Lisa looked up from her desk and squealed. "Come in, come in."

Riley did, closing the door behind her so she could have ten minutes to talk without being overheard. Plus, Lisa's office was closer to Hope's, and the owner of the company was in this afternoon.

She handed Lisa the file and sank onto the couch in the office. "I need your honest opinion."

"Would I ever give you anything less?" Lisa left the file on her desk and came around it to sit in the armchair across from Riley. "But let me guess first. You're worried about why he's interested in you. Like, how is that even possible?" She cocked her head, her blue eyes looking right through Riley's soul. "Right?"

"Yes," Riley said, glad Lisa had said it so she didn't have to. "I mean, you know who he is, right?"

"The Sexiest Man Alive in 2016," Lisa said. "The *world* knows who he is."

"Exactly," Riley said, her insecurities rearing up. She played with the ends of her hair, which wasn't all real. Since striking out so often, she'd decided she just needed a change. It was easy to dye her hair and put in extensions. She'd started watching makeup videos online, and she had a much more dramatic look now.

"You're amazing," Lisa said. "And he obviously saw it. I mean, the man knows greatness when he sees it, right?"

"Or maybe he's delusional," Riley said. "Or desperate." She sighed and leaned back against the couch, closing her eyes. "He doesn't live here. What if I'm just setting myself up to get my heart broken?"

Lisa remained quiet for a few seconds. "Okay," she finally said. "Let's say you only get to be with him for a month. Wouldn't you want those thirty days? Or would you rather not have him at all?"

"You're too practical," Riley said.

"And you're too wrapped up in thinking ten miles down the road."

"Ouch." Riley sat up and looked at her friend, who

wore a stern yet sympathetic look on her face. "But okay. I can give you that one."

Lisa smiled at her and got up to come sit beside her on the couch. "I'd take the thirty days, Riley. Or ten. Or whatever that man has to give, because he's the *Sexiest Man Alive*." She started laughing, and Riley couldn't help joining in.

"Okay," Riley said, drawing in a deep breath. "We're going to dinner tonight. You know my wardrobe. What do I wear?"

"For a man who might only be in your life for a few days? The sexiest thing you own—that little black number with the pink heels."

"I can barely walk in those," Riley said.

"Exactly," Lisa said with another giggle, lacing her arm through Riley's. "So you just *have* to hold onto Evan."

"Lisa?" someone said into the intercom on her phone, and Riley jumped.

"Your appointment." Horror snaked through her, because that sounded like Hope's voice. And Hope really hated it when their clients came into the building and someone wasn't there to greet them, offer them a drink, and personally deliver them to their consultants. In fact, that was Riley's job.

Sure enough, Hope said, "Gillian is here. I'll bring her back."

"Thank you," Lisa said in a normal voice, having jumped to her feet. She strode to the door and whispered, "Go. Hurry. And call me when you get home, no matter how late it is."

Riley slipped by her and down the hall and into the kitchen. She could say she was in the restroom, not getting free counseling from her best friend. She waited until she heard Lisa say, "Gillian, hello. Thank you, Hope," before she left the kitchen and returned to her desk, her thoughts already back on her outfit and jewelry for her date that night.

RILEY WAS READY A FEW MINUTES EARLY, BUT SHE DIDN'T put her shoes on yet. She was still undecided if the five-inch heels were appropriate. Maybe she'd wait and ask Evan what he had in mind for that night. Maybe they'd be strolling along the beach. Maybe he'd booked them at a luau. Maybe everything she currently wore would need to change.

Because she looked like she was going to a freaking pageant. Crystal dripped from her earlobes and she'd pulled the sides of her hair back into an elaborate set of curls pinned to the crown of her head. Plenty of hair still hung over her shoulders, which were bare as this dress didn't even have a spaghetti strap.

The dress was form-fitting and fell to just above her knee in a shiny, flirty, fun fabric that hid the fact that she counted walking up and down the halls at Your Tidal Forever as an exercise plan.

The doorbell rang, and she jumped away from the fridge, where she'd been staring for at least five minutes.

Marbles meowed and ran toward the door as if Riley hadn't heard the bell. Sunshine looked at her from the cat bed in the kitchen, almost like, *is the door for you or me?*

"Come on," she said to the cat. "You'll like this guy." Some people had cats that hid whenever someone came over, but Riley's acted more like aloof fathers. They needed to check out each visitor and give their approval.

So each feline arrived at the door before her, and Marbles stretched up on his back feet as if he could reach the door with his front paws.

Riley opened the door, her heart pounding in the back of her throat, making swallowing and breathing and talking difficult.

Evan stood there, looking absolutely stunning in a casual pair of dark gray slacks and a dark purple dress shirt, open at the throat. The inky ends of a tattoo on his chest peeked out from underneath the shirt, and Riley liked seeing only part of it as much as witnessing the whole thing.

"Look at you," he said, scanning her body from her toes to her eyes. "How'd I get lucky enough to get you to go out with me?" He grinned like he was truly happy to see her, and Riley could do one thing with the ball of emotions stuck in her throat.

She smiled.

Chapter Six

Evan had never seen a more beautiful woman. And when she smiled like that, he couldn't even remember his own name.

"I need help with the shoes," she said.

"Is that so?"

"You never said where we were going." She waved for him to come inside her house, so he stepped from porch to front room. Two cats immediately pressed against his legs, and he bent down and chuckled.

"Hey, guys," he said. "Let's see if I can get your names right. Marbles," he said to the gray and black cat. "And Sunshine must be the white and orange one." He glanced up at Riley, who giggled.

"You got it."

He straightened and reached for her hand, unable to keep his to himself for another moment. He felt like someone had sprinkled a heavy amount of pixie dust over him, and everything was so magical. The woman. Her cats. The sound of her voice. All of it.

"So I like to wear these really high heels with this dress," she said. "But I wasn't sure if we were going somewhere where more practical shoes would be appropriate."

"I had the concierge at Sweet Breeze pick our place," he said. "It's on the North Shore."

"Oh, so more casual." Riley toed a pair of wedges that weren't as high but would surely be as sexy as the heels.

"Is the North Shore more casual?" he asked.

"Definitely," Riley said. "Tons of surfing up there, and way less tourists."

"That's what I requested—the less tourists part."

She bent to begin putting on the white wedges, but Evan really wanted to see the heels. "Let's see the pink heels first," he said.

"Yeah?" She stepped easily into those, and Evan forgot his own name.

His mouth turned dry, and he quickly pulled his phone from his pocket. "Maybe I need a picture to compare. Strike a pose for me."

Riley looked at him for a few seconds, the silence turning awkward. "Really?"

"Why not? Don't tell me a woman like you doesn't know how to pose." He grinned at her and swiped his camera on.

Riley smiled and put one hand on her hip, pushing it

out. Evan backed up to make sure he got the heels and snapped the picture. "Okay, the white ones."

She put those on, which took a bit longer due to the straps around the back of her heel. She struck the same pose, and Evan took another picture. "Okay, stay there," he said, bringing up the one with the pink heels. He held the phone out and looked at her in the flesh and her in the picture, wearing the pink heels.

"Honestly, I think it's the pink heels, Riley." He really liked saying her name, and he could not imagine ending this date without kissing her. She had all the curves he liked on a woman, and all that hair.... He wanted to fist his fingers in it while he held her close. While they danced on the beach to a band only they could hear.

Slow down, he told himself. Carl told him he was too romantic about things, but Evan didn't know how to be any different. He wrote a ton of songs about relationships and love—how else was he supposed to be?

"Can I hold onto your arm if I wear them?" she asked. "Because they're high, and I have a feeling I'm going to want you to take me to the beach after dinner."

"You like the beach?" Evan wanted to know everything about this woman.

"Love it," she said. "When the moon is up, and the breeze is blowing, and there's a handsome man on my arm...." She gave him a coy smile and changed her shoes. With the pink heels back on, she said, "All right, rockstar. I'm ready."

Evan held out his arm, and pure electricity pulsed

through him in the few moments it took Riley to cross the space between them and link her arm in his. "So where are we going tonight?"

"We have a private booth at Oceanside," he said, leading her out onto the porch.

"Stay," she said to the gray cat, and he meowed mournfully at her. "Oh, you're fine. I'll be back later, Marbles."

Evan chuckled as Riley closed the door behind them. The ends of her hair brushed his forearm, and pure pleasure moved through him.

"Oh, you have a car service," Riley said, clear surprise in her voice.

"I don't have a car on the island," he said. "I actually don't like cars much."

"Really?" She paused as he opened the car door for her and looked into his eyes.

He could look at her forever, and he worked to calm his pulse. He felt this rush every time he stepped on a stage, and if he could have it in his personal life too, he really wanted it.

"Someone like you, with lots of money? Tell me you don't own at least three cars."

"I don't own at least three cars."

"How many do you own?"

"Two." He grinned at her. "Now, motorcycles...I have a few of those."

"And how many is a few for Evan Garfield?" she teased.

Evan tipped his head back and laughed, the sound flying up into the sky. "Six."

"Six?" Riley shook her head, everything about her speaking to Evan's soul. "Evan, the term you're looking for is several. You have *several* motorcycles."

"No," he argued in good fun. "I'd need *seven* to get to *several*. Six is still a few."

"We'll agree to disagree." She slid into the car, and Evan followed her, glad she didn't move too far over on the seat. In fact, she cuddled right into him the way he'd fantasized about earlier that day.

He laced his fingers through hers, unable to keep his smile from spreading across his whole face. "So we don't agree about counting terms," he said. "But I love the beach too, so that's one thing in common. And I'm excited to tell you I got a place here in Getaway Bay."

"You did?" Riley turned her head and looked at him. "You're renting?"

"Yep," he said. "For several months."

"Oh, boy." The flirtation in her voice made everything male in him come alive. "There's that several again."

"I signed a six-month contract."

"So six *is* several."

"I walked into this one, didn't I?" He laughed, glad when Riley joined him. "A friend of mine is getting married here on the island in December, and he called this afternoon to ask if I'd sing at the wedding."

"Oh, really? Which wedding is it?"

"His name is Charlie Pyne. His fiancée is Amelia Webb."

"Pyne?" Riley's perfectly sculpted eyebrows lifted. "We're planning that wedding. I mean, I'm not. My firm. Your Tidal Forever."

"Oh, that's amazing."

"His consultant is one of my best friends," Riley said, beaming at him. "Lisa Ashford. Amelia is local to Getaway Bay. I think she met Charlie…let's see. On a camping trip in Canada?"

"Yeah." Evan marveled at her. "How do you remember all of that?"

"It's my *job* to know all of that," she said. "I'm supposed to know every person who walks through the door and have earl grey tea ready for some and hot coffee for others, cold soda for certain brides, and only filtered water for still others."

"I can barely remember what I did yesterday," Evan said, the smooth movement of the car beneath him comforting.

"You remembered me," she said. "Enough to remember I worked at a wedding planning company."

"True," he said. "I suppose if I'm motivated enough, I can recall details." He remembered a lot of things that had happened in his forty-two years of life. The important things. The events and people that really mattered.

Like Riley.

He squeezed her hand. "Thanks for going out with me."

"You can surely get a date anytime you want," she said.

"I don't know about that."

"Oh, jeez." She rolled her eyes. "Do you even know who you are?"

"Do you?"

Riley looked at him again, their eyes locking. Several seconds of silence passed, and Evan didn't know her very well, but he wanted to know everything he could.

"Behind all of the awards, and the songs, and the titles, I'm just Evan Garfield," he said. "And the sooner you realize that, the more fun we'll be able to have."

Riley drew in a deep breath, so many things swirling in those gorgeous, green eyes. "Okay, if you're just a regular guy, tell me something you did as a kid to get into trouble."

Evan started chuckling, the sound turning into laughter pretty quickly. "That's an easy one. I'm the oldest of three brothers, and I'm pretty sure no one in Sweet Springs was upset when the Garfields moved."

"So you led the charge into mischief," Riley said.

"All the time," Evan said. "One time, we went and picked all the peas from our neighbor's garden down the street. I *loved* fresh peas from the garden." Evan could smell the night air, feel the dirt beneath his bare feet, and taste those fresh peas. "We'd done it too many times, and he was waiting for us. With a gun." Evan laughed again, though he hadn't been laughing then. "We got in so much trouble. My dad actually called the cops on us."

"Your dad? Not the neighbor?"

"Kent Shirtluff called my dad. My dad called the cops. Lessons were learned. All that jazz."

"So you didn't raid people's gardens anymore."

"Well...." Evan laughed again, cutting off the sound after only a moment. "Carl really liked tomatoes from the garden."

"Why didn't you guys just plant your own dang garden?" Riley laughed too, and Evan couldn't believe what his life had become in such a short time.

"Gardens require work," he said. "Why do all that when you can sneak over a fence in the middle of the night?"

"You're bad," she said, still giggling.

"Hey, I've never been arrested," he said. "And that's something when you're a celebrity."

"I'll take your word for it," she said dryly.

"Hey, do you want to go shopping with me tomorrow?" he asked.

"What are you buying?" she asked.

"A motorcycle."

She sighed as she leaned back into his body. "You really are a bad boy, even if the law hasn't caught up to you yet."

Hey, if she wanted a bad boy, Evan could be that for her.

Chapter Seven

Riley glanced around Oceanside as Evan stepped up to the hostess station. It was definitely a high-end restaurant, right on the beach, with a pretty cool vibe. Most of the North Shore had a relaxed, laid-back vibe, with more people in Hawaiian shirts than suits and ties.

Or no shirts at all.

"Right this way," the woman said, and Evan reached for Riley's hand again. She followed him through the restaurant, which had ritzy music playing and fancy lighting on the tables.

They had a booth overlooking the ocean, and since it wasn't terribly late yet, the sunlight spilling through the windows lit up this part of the restaurant. The half-moon shaped table had a curved booth behind it, with just enough room for two people.

Riley slid in before Evan, but she didn't give him much room, just like she hadn't in the car. She liked the heat of his body right beside her, the touch of his hand against her bare knee as he held his menu with one hand, the way he smiled to himself.

She looked at the menu too, in a desperate attempt to distract herself and give herself a moment to calm down. He really was handsome, and she'd really enjoyed his childhood stories on the car ride here, and she liked that he just wanted to be seen as a normal man.

No one here had even looked at him twice, and he'd been smart to come up to the North Shore. "Do you like fish?" she asked him, and he shook his head slightly.

"I mean, yeah," he said. "Not as much as steak, I guess. Or pasta. I have a real weakness for pasta."

"Really? I would not have guessed that about you."

Evan looked away from his menu. "What would you have guessed?"

The waitress arrived, saving her from having to answer immediately. "Drinks for you two?" she asked.

Evan looked at Riley, and she said, "I want something fruity and slushy, without the alcohol."

"We have a few mocktails," the waitress said, indicating the back of the menu. "I recommend the Getaway Bay Berry. It's tart and sweet and refreshing."

"I'll take that," Riley said, looking at Evan.

"Diet Coke with lemon," he said. "And water."

"Be right back." The waitress moved away, and Riley looked back at her menu, well aware that Evan did not.

"What would you have guessed my favorite food was?" he asked.

"Pizza?" she guessed.

He chuckled and nodded. "A fair assessment."

"Plus, I read it when I looked at your Sexiest Man Alive article."

"Oh-ho," he said, focusing on his menu again. "I'm going to get the trout."

"And I'm going to get the beef bolognese," she said. "Did you know there's a cattle ranch here on the island?"

"There is?" The innocent, vibrant look in his eyes made Riley smile.

"There sure is. We should go horseback riding out there. Do rockstars go horseback riding?"

"This one does," he said, reaching for his drink the moment the waitress set it on the table.

"Ready to order?" she asked.

Evan started rattling off a couple of appetizers, ending with his choice of the trout. Riley opened her mouth to order, but Evan put in her order too, and warmth filled her from head to toe. He was full of class and sophistication, as well as a fun, flirty streak that made Riley feel reckless.

She still had no idea why he liked her, but she remembered her conversation with Lisa from earlier that day. Even if Evan was only here for six months, Riley wanted them to be the most spectacular *several* months of her life.

"I LOVE THE STARS," SHE TOLD HIM LATER THAT NIGHT, AS they walked along the beach. He carried her heels in one hand, and she still held onto his arm with both of her hands. "You can see The Big Dipper over there."

"I see it," he said, his voice quiet under the wide blanket of sky above them. "And Orion's belt. I think that's the only one I know."

"Me too," she said. "But I like getting out of the city and looking at the stars from time to time."

"I love staying up late," he said. "And sleeping late. Drives my brother crazy."

"So you like motorcycles, fresh peas, trout, steak, cats, dogs, diet soda, the beach, and staying up late." Riley knew there was much more to him than just these things, and their dinner conversation had been the typical fare for a real first date.

Or second.

Or was this their third?

Riley was going to go with the third date, and she wondered if it was too early to kiss him. The sand squished beneath her feet, and the sound of the waves crashing against the shore several paces to her right made for the most magical setting.

But she still felt like most of what she'd told him—and what he'd told her—was superficial. Surface stuff. And she did want to have a fun time with him for as long as he was on the island of Getaway Bay. But she didn't need to carve out her own heart and hand it to him on a platter.

So she put an additional six inches of space between them and told him a story about something her cats had done the previous week.

Everything was light and fun and romantic, and Riley didn't want to ruin it. The hour approached midnight by the time the car service pulled up to her house. Evan walked her to the front door, and Riley keyed in her lock code before turning to face him.

"I have to work tomorrow, and you can't take me for a two-hour lunch." She reached over and fiddled with the collar on his shirt.

Evan held very still, smiling at her. "What time do you get off?"

"Usually five or six, depending on what's going on."

"And you get an hour-long lunch?"

"That's right, rockstar."

"So we'll have an hour for lunch together, and then after work, you can come help me buy a motorcycle."

"Help you?" Riley flirted with him shamelessly. "I'm not putting down the down payment."

He chuckled and ducked his head. "I need a mode of transportation for the island, and a motorcycle seems like the best option. Maybe I just want to know which one you'd like to ride on the back of."

"And I get to pick out a helmet," she said.

"There's that too." Evan put his arms around her and brought her close. His heart thumped steadily in his chest, reverberating through her eardrums and making her pulse match his. "I had a great time tonight. Thanks for treating me like a regular guy."

He was anything but a regular guy, but in that moment, standing with him on her front porch after a great date, Riley had to admit that this felt normal.

Riley stepped back and heard Marbles meowing behind the door. "Lunch is at twelve-thirty, rockstar. Don't be late." She opened the door and slipped inside, proud of herself for not kissing him and not swallowing what she wanted to say.

His laughter was the last thing she heard as the door closed, and then she leaned against it, a sigh coming out of her mouth.

"Well," she said, dropping her shoes on the floor near the front door. "That was one of the best dates *ever.*" She scooped Sunshine into her arms and moved further into the house. "What have you guys been doing?"

Neither cat responded, and once Riley had peeled her dress off and put on her pajamas, she sat in bed with both cats curled up beside her. Lisa's phone only rang once before she picked up with the words, "Tell me everything."

"Okay, I'm going to start with what's worrying me," Riley said. "And then you can hear the stories and tell me if I'm right or not."

"Talk fast, girl. We have to be to work in the morning."

Riley knew. She wasn't a night-owl like Evan, and she smothered a yawn in order to say, "I'm worried he's a little too perfect."

"Oh, honey, you can't worry about that at this point," Lisa said. "Of course he's too perfect right now. It's what? Your second date?"

"Yeah," Riley said, glad she hadn't kissed him. The meeting in the coffee shop wasn't a real date, and she shouldn't be counting it as one. He'd been there to get his watch; nothing more.

"So you're still in the honeymoon phase. He's not going to show all his flaws for a while."

"Do you think he really has them?" Riley asked.

"Everyone does, Riley."

"I know," she said. "He just looks so good online."

"Everyone looks good online," Lisa said. "Have you seen our pictures on the Forever website? The photographer slimmed out my face and it looks like I weigh twenty pounds less than I actually do." Lisa started laughing, though if she really lost twenty pounds, she'd blow away.

Riley laughed too, because she was right. Hope had wanted near glamour shots, and a couple of the consultants even had their hair blowing as if they needed a headshot for a dating website and not their wedding planning company staff page.

"All right," she said. "But he really is the sexiest man alive."

"Did you kiss him?" Lisa asked.

"Lise," Riley said in mock horror.

"What? I haven't been on a date in six months."

Riley's heart pinched, and she sobered. "I know, honey. But you'll find someone, I just know it."

"Yeah, I'm going to join Getaway Bay Singles. I've been putting it off long enough, and I need a boyfriend for my family's holiday party. I am *not* going alone again."

Riley had tried the island dating app as well, and she had gotten a lot of dates. She was sure some people found lasting relationships using the app, but she'd found a lot of the men she'd gone out with weren't looking to commit. They just wanted a few dinners, and then they moved on.

Or maybe she was just only good for a few dates before a man got bored. She wasn't sure which. What she knew was that she'd deactivated her account, taken a break from going out, and reinvented her look.

"It can take almost twenty-five dates before you find a keeper," Riley said.

"Don't remind me," Lisa groaned. "Okay, I'm getting off with you and getting on that app. Might as well get the first date over with."

Riley laughed and their call ended. She wondered if she'd have caught Evan's eye with her usually reddish-brown hair and fresh-faced look. What if he'd have looked right past her? Or at least just asked for his watch and left?

Stop thinking about it, she told herself. Evan had told her once that he didn't do what-ifs, and she needed to be more like him in that regard.

Maybe then she could be perfect too.

Chapter Eight

Evan liked to shower every day. He wasn't sure why, only that he thrived on routine, and that included a shower every morning when he got up. Fine, sometimes he woke up in the afternoon, depending on how late he'd been up the night before.

Sweet Breeze Resort and Spa had plenty to do after the sun went down, and he'd enjoyed a concert on the beach after dropping Riley off that took him past midnight. And if there was a better time to eat sliders and drink ice cold cola, he didn't want to know about it.

The next morning, he woke after only five hours of sleep, because he needed time to get ready and get over to Your Tidal Forever to pick up Riley.

Giddiness pranced through him as he lay in bed, and that same feeling propelled him out from under the blankets and into the shower. He sang while he washed, and when he stepped out, his brother knocked on his door.

"Just getting out of the shower," he called, tucking his towel around his waist. "Come in." He liked dealing with Carl in the morning too, as his brother was usually a little less surly after coffee and before interacting with too many people.

The house Evan had rented was huge, and he heard Carl's footsteps several seconds before he arrived in the cavernous bathroom. It was all done in white and gray tiles, marble on the countertops, and sleek, modern glass for the mirrors and shower. But it echoed like a cave, and Evan thought an entire troop of Boy Scouts could live in the bathroom for days and no one would find them.

"A reporter out of LA wants a quote," he said, appearing with a clipboard in his hand. "You have a ten-thirty brunch with the billionaire group tomorrow." He glanced up as Evan opened the drawer in the vanity to pull out his toothbrush. "And Brett called to say Mom wants us home for Thanksgiving."

Evan squeezed toothpaste onto his brush and got it wet. He said, "I can do Thanksgiving," to which Carl groaned. Evan smiled anyway. "The brunch is fine. I'll have to get to bed early tonight." Which totally wasn't happening. He had a date with Riley, and he wanted every second he could get from her. "And what's the quote for?"

He started brushing his teeth as Carl started rambling about some article someone was doing on the rise of male vocalists. "You've got that interview you did about eight months ago," he said. "I could pull from that."

"Great," Evan said with a mouth full of foam. He spat and rinsed and grinned at Carl. "You don't want to go home for Thanksgiving?"

"Not particularly."

"Why not?" Evan watched his brother, because he knew Carl's tells better than anyone. Sometimes even better than Carl himself.

"I just don't." He turned around and walked away. "But I'll tell Brett we can make it."

Evan chuckled to himself, thinking he knew exactly why Carl didn't want to go back to Green Grove, Georgia: a woman. One specific woman, who'd broken his brother's heart. When Carl's relationship with Shay had ended, Evan had brought him on full-time as the band's manager. Brett was already working with Georgia Panic on songwriting and doing a few bookings.

Carl had taken things to a new level. Nothing the man did was finished halfway, something Evan appreciated. Plus, his new job got Carl out of Green Grove and away from Shay. It had been a win for everyone.

Twenty minutes later, Evan emerged from the master suite and headed across the lobby of the house into the kitchen. Carl worked at the counter there, though he sometimes took his papers out to the pool if it wasn't too windy.

"I'm headed out," Evan said, plucking the keys to the car they'd rented from the hook beside the garage door.

"I'll catch a ride down to wherever you buy your bike," he said without looking up. Evan simply smiled at him, though he wanted to tell him he wasn't buying a bike. He was purchasing a motorcycle, and there was a big difference between the two.

But Carl had most likely said that on purpose, and Evan didn't feel like arguing, at least not right now. He'd usually go toe-to-toe with his brother, and with Brett not here to break things up, the argument could be epic.

Instead he said, "Don't wait up for me," and opened the door.

"You have a brunch at ten-thirty!" Carl yelled after him. Evan let the door slam behind him, a very final punctuation mark on the sentence.

He could attend a brunch a little tired. Heck, he was tired now, and he was going on a date with a woman he cared about a whole lot more than a bunch of stuffy billionaires.

He pulled up to Your Tidal Forever twenty minutes early and got out of the car though the air was stifling and hot. There wasn't much of a breeze behind the buildings, and he walked down the quaint boardwalk to the other side. The sand stretched before him, with the beautiful water extending beyond that. A sense of wonder filled him, and he was glad he'd ended the tour here.

Glad he'd stayed. Even if he hadn't met Riley, this was the perfect place for him right now. Everything was so…slow. And slow was exactly what Evan needed.

His phone rang, and he swiped on the call from Riley eagerly. "Hey, babe," he said.

"Babe?" She didn't sound like she appreciated that. "Okay, since you're a world-famous rockstar, I'm going to let that slide. Just. Once."

He chuckled, but her point had been driven home quite nicely. "Second, you don't have to lurk out on the boardwalk. You can come inside. I'm not done for a few more minutes."

"I wasn't lurking," he said. "I just got here, and it was too hot behind the building."

"It's too hot everywhere," she said. "And you totally look like a creeper. Come inside." Someone said her name on the other end of the line, and she said, "Gotta go," and hung up.

Lurking. Creeper. He wasn't doing either of those things, but he sure did like hearing Riley's voice. Their texting string went on for miles, too, and she'd included a picture or two, usually of some colored folders and her explanation for how she did her job.

Evan found everything about her fascinating, right down to the fact that she'd once had three holes in her ears and then let two of them grow in. A lot of rockstars had piercings, but Evan hadn't seen the allure. No, for him, it was all about the ink. He had half a dozen tattoos, most of them small and meaningful to him.

He rubbed his right fingers along the edge of his left hand, where he had a series of stars to signify his dreaming spirit. He loved to look at the stars, and he loved to wish on them, even now as a grown man.

Turning toward the building where Your Tidal

Forever was housed, he tilted his head back and looked into the sky. "No stars visible right now," he murmured, though he knew they were still out there.

So he wished that he and Riley could have an amazing afternoon together and walked over to the entrance. She looked up from her desk and grinned at him, jumping out of her seat a moment later.

"Hey, rockstar," she said.

"Hey, gorgeous." He received her into his arms, and she didn't reprimand him for the endearment this time. She giggled and he chuckled, and it was as if lightning had struck right there in the lobby of her workplace.

Everything inside him sizzled and snapped, and Evan really, *really* liked this woman. She stepped back, those straight, white teeth framed by daring, red lips. "So babe is bad," he said. "But gorgeous is okay."

"Babe is a pig in a children's movie," she said. "All uses of how amazing and stunning I am are acceptable." She flipped her dark hair over her shoulder with a flirtatious look in her eye and headed back to her desk. "I have maybe fifteen more things to do before we can go."

"Oh, only fifteen, huh?"

"Don't worry. I'll be ready on time." She pointed to a posh white couch, which clearly only supermodels and Persian cats had sat on. "You can wait right there."

Yeah, if he wanted to have a kinked back by the time they left. Still, there wasn't anywhere else to wait, and he didn't think hovering over her was a good idea. Riley was smart and competent, as well as the best flirter he'd been out with in a long time.

The couch had a glass coffee table in front of it, holding various magazines and even a couple of newspapers. He picked up the Getaway Bay Gazette, startled to see his picture on the front page. The other members of Georgia Panic stood behind him, the five of them making a V-shape with him as the lead goose.

He looked fierce with his arms folded and his face so stony. Did this man ever smile? That was surely what people thought when they looked at him.

The headline read *Georgia Panic sweeps nation, ends tour in Getaway Bay*. So far, so good. Evan had learned long ago not to read articles about himself or the band. Only about half of it was true, and even that half depended on who someone asked.

Southern gentlemen in black leather caught his eye, and he thought that was a decent way to describe the band. As was *they are rock, pop, and soul all in one, with a front man who's as charismatic as he is talented.*

Okay, so maybe he could read more articles about himself and the band.

It was always interesting to see how others perceived him, and he glanced over to where Riley worked. She had her phone at her ear, talking while she tapped out something on her computer. She typed, she shuffled, she filed.

And five minutes later, she turned everything off and rose from her chair. "Ready?"

Evan was mesmerized by this woman, so he could only nod as he stood up.

"Great, so we're buying a motorcycle, and then we're going to dinner."

"Right." He lifted his arm around her. "But we'll probably ride the motorcycle to dinner. You can get on a machine in that?" He let his gaze slide down her body to the tapering pencil skirt that brushed the tops of her knees.

"I guess we'll find out," she said with a smile. "And you can drop me off here after."

He didn't really like the sound of that. He wanted to walk her to the door, the hum of the motorcycle's engine still in his blood, and kiss her goodnight. Would she let him?

He put the question out of his mind for now. All of them, from how she could climb on a motorcycle in that skirt to where they'd eat dinner to how their night would end.

He'd find out soon enough.

They chatted easily on the way to the motorcycle dealership, whom he'd already called and asked them to be ready for him. Sure, maybe it was a diva thing to do, but he wanted to buy a motorcycle in less than an hour. He had cash. He just needed to find one he liked.

"Here we are," he said, opening the door for her. Riley entered first, and she looked like someone straight out of a magazine. He followed, and he was definitely the rocker with the devil-may-care attitude.

He wore jeans and black boots and a T-shirt with his band's name on the front. In fact, he couldn't remember the last time he'd worn anything but something very similar to what he had on now.

"Hello," a man said. "You must be Evan Garfield."

"Guilty," Evan said, shaking the man's hand.

"I'm Juan, and I'll be helping you today."

"This is Riley," Evan said. "Her opinion matters a whole lot." He grinned at her as she shook her head and smiled. He felt like he'd swallowed sparkles, and she definitely wore stars in her eyes.

"Great." Juan shook her hand too. "I think I know you...."

"Have you or someone you know been married recently?" She cocked her head slightly, as if trying to see inside Juan's mind.

"Yes, my cousin."

"She probably used Your Tidal Forever," Riley said. "I work there."

"She did." Juan smiled. "She had a great wedding planner...Shannon, I think?"

"Shannon is fantastic," Riley said, oh-so-diplomatically. Evan could watch her in this role forever, but he really wanted to find out what she was like on the back of a bike.

A motorcycle, he corrected himself mentally.

"Okay," Juan said, moving on. "I have here that you want something with power. I've got a few things for you to look at." He started across the showroom floor, and Evan caught Riley's hand in his.

"He has notes on you already?" Riley asked.

"I may have called ahead," Evan said.

"You may have called ahead," she repeated dryly. "Wow, the life of the rich and famous."

Evan wasn't sure if he should be offended by that or simply laugh. Riley wasn't giving him any clues with her facial expression, so he just nodded. "That's right, *babe.* And you get to see it firsthand."

"Oh, you didn't," she said.

"Oh, I did." He paused next to a motorcycle on the showroom floor, only a couple of paces from Juan.

"This is our newest arrival," Juan said. "It's an X-Diavel from Ducati. It's part cruiser, as you can see. But it's got great power and style."

Oh, this motorcycle had style all right. A whole lot of style.

"It seats two," Juan said.

Very important.

"And you won't feel like you're weighed down with this bike."

Evan circled it and nodded. "I want to drive it."

"Right now? Or would you like to see what else we have?"

"Let's see what else you have," Evan said. "But I definitely want to try this one." He shot a smile at Riley, who looked at the motorcycle like it was a monster from the great deep. Working with everything he had, he managed not to laugh.

This night was going to be so much fun.

Chapter Nine

Riley could not imagine a worse wardrobe choice for motorcycle riding. She didn't understand all of the words Juan and Evan said, but she knew enough to realize the words were foreign. And expensive.

Her experience with motorcycles was really with motor *scooters*, and there was a vast difference between the pretty pastel vehicles she saw zipping around the island and this sexy, black, muscly motorcycle. Evan kept looking at it like he was starving and it was his next meal.

"So you've got two you want to try," Juan said after about twenty minutes of walking around.

"The Ducati," Evan said. "And this Harley."

At least Riley had heard of a Harley Davidson. Maybe she hadn't heard of all the letters and numbers in the one Juan had shown to them, but she did like the pretty, Hawaiian paint job on that other bike.

But this black and chrome Ducati....

"...needs a helmet too," Evan said, and Riley tuned back into the conversation.

"This way," Juan said, and Riley wasn't exactly sure what she'd missed. It all became clear though, as they approached a wall of helmets. Literally, a wall. She stared blankly at it, because she had no idea how to tackle something like this.

"Do you know what size?" Juan asked, and Riley turned her head toward him as if in slow motion.

"I'm a large," Evan said, glancing at Riley. "I'm guessing she's a medium."

"We have full-face helmets, open face, or half," Juan said, looking from Riley to Evan expectantly. "Our off-road items are down on the end, but I don't think that's what you want."

Riley thought he was speaking English, but it was really hard to tell right now.

"I like the open concept," Evan said, looking at her. "What about you, babe?"

She growled at him, because she did not like being called *babe*. His eyes laughed at her, and dang if that playful smile didn't make her heart race and the temperature at the helmet wall go up at least ten degrees.

"That's a half," Juan said. "And those are down here."

"What does all this mean?" she hissed to Evan as he took a couple of steps after Juan.

"You'll probably like a full-face or an open face," he

said. "See how these go all the way around your face? That's a full-face helmet. The open face just doesn't have the front part." He took the matte black helmet Juan handed to him. "And this one is a half, which is more old-school."

He put it on and started fiddling with the straps, transforming him from the Sexiest Man Alive to the Sexiest Man in the Universe. Or the Sexiest Man Among All Living and Dead.

Something.

Juan looked at her, and said, "I have some great female full-face helmets. Did you have a color preference?" He reminded her so much of herself, what with how efficient and professional he was.

"Yes." She cleared her throat. "My favorite color is pink."

Evan made a noise halfway between a cough and a scoff, his eyes devouring her as she accepted the bright pink, full-face helmet from Juan. She pushed it on, immediately feeling like she was about to combust.

Evan stepped over to her and started helping her with the straps. "Oh, this is nice," he said, his eyes flitting everywhere besides looking at hers. He buckled the chinstrap and tightened it, the padding actually quite soft against her neck.

He did look at her then, and every cell liquefied under that sexy, intense gaze. "So nice." He stepped back as if he'd just told her what time it was and looked at Juan. "We're ready."

"I'll get the keys to the Ducati." Juan walked away, and panic built inside Riley fully.

Evan reached for her hand and led her back to the showroom floor. Every step soothed her—until another salesman approached and said, "Ma'am, you can't ride in those shoes."

She looked at her two-inch heels—completely appropriate for her job. But not for riding motorcycles.

"You can wear these." He handed her a box with a brand new pair of boots in them. Black boots. Riley frowned, but she moved over to the chairs and laced up. By then, Juan had returned, and it was almost time to ride.

He talked to Evan about the controls, the weight of the bike, the handlebars, passenger weight, all of it. Riley stood there, wondering how on Earth she was going to get on the back of that thing. The motorcycle looked more like a death trap than anything else.

Evan swung one leg over it effortlessly, and suddenly, the Ducati took on a new life. A new personality. He looked at her over his shoulder. "Climb on, beautiful. Let's see how she handles."

Riley looked at him and then the tiny backseat behind him. She looked down at her skirt. With nothing else to do, she stepped over to the bike, hitched up her skirt, and swung her leg over the seat too.

To her great surprise, she landed behind him, her arms easily snaking around him and holding on tight. "Oh, wow," she said.

Evan chuckled, the vibrations from his voice box shimmying through her whole body. "Wow is right. I wish I had that on video."

"Stop it," she said. "And don't kill us."

He started the bike, the roar of it making Riley cringe at the same time excitement poured through her. The vehicle rumbled beneath her, and then Evan said, "Here we go." He eased them to moving, lifting his own booted feet off the ground after several yards. Shockingly, the bike stayed balanced, and he drove them to the exit.

"Okay, babe," he said. "You have to lean with me on turns, okay?"

"If you call me babe one more time…."

He laughed, painting the sky with his delicious voice. "Okay, sorry. But you really do have to lean with me, Riley."

Oh, saying her name was no fair. She nodded and said, "Okay. Lean with you."

"Just press right into me, sweetheart. Go with my body."

She wanted to go wherever he was, so she leaned in further, and pressed right into him the way he'd said.

"Good girl," he said, and normally that would've really irked Riley. Maybe it was the fumes from the motorcycle exhaust. Or maybe she'd gone crazy. Or maybe being fused to Evan had fried her brain cells.

Either way, he moved them forward again, leaned to the right, and she went along with him.

A few turns later, and he was on the coastal highway,

driving fast and leaning around corners. Riley held on, moved with him, breathed, and enjoyed the ride.

When they got back, she dismounted from the bike by holding onto one of Juan's hands while Evan steadied the bike.

"What did you think?" Juan asked.

"That was amazing," she said breathlessly. "Absolutely amazing." She sucked at the air, her adrenaline still soaring somewhere in the stratosphere.

"I think he was asking me, sweetheart." Evan kicked a smile in her direction and said, "I'm buying that."

"You haven't ridden the Harley Davidson."

"It won't be better than that," he said. "Let's go get this done. I'm starving."

An hour later, Riley dismounted from the bike by herself, Evan doing the same right behind her. "You like it, don't you?" He took her helmet from her and stowed it on the handlebars, which were about as wide as the seat she'd ridden on.

He already knew she liked it. "I'm glad they put on that extra bar," she said. "That seat is tiny, especially behind you."

Evan slung his arm around her shoulders, and she felt like a dwarf compared to him. "You just lean into me, baby."

"Maybe I want to see where I'm going," she said.

"I can have them put on the extra-long seat." He looked at her, his eyebrows raised.

If she said yes, she'd be admitting that she'd be riding this bike around the island with him. If she said no…she didn't want to say no. "I think you should do that," she said as they reached the door for the Cattleman's Last Stop. It wasn't fancy food, but it was good, and Evan liked hamburgers. She'd learned that from their texting fests.

"Consider it done," he said, holding the door for her.

They went inside, and the hostess said, "Pick a table, you two."

Riley chose one in the corner so Evan could sit with his back to the door, which he did. "The servings here are huge."

"Good," he said as he picked up the menu already on the table. "I really am hungry."

"Can you afford dinner after buying that bike?" she asked innocently. "I mean, it seems like your wallet should be really empty by now." He'd just plunked down almost thirty thousand dollars for that motorcycle—and he hadn't even blinked.

"Not as empty as my stomach," he said without looking up. Code for *nope, not out of money yet*. Riley understood a lot of codes. "What are you getting?" He did look at her then, and she hadn't even picked up a menu. "Do you come here a lot?"

"Yes," she said simply. "It's a very popular place for first dates."

Evan blinked, his show of surprise. "I think we're on four or five."

"You think we're on four or five?" Riley laughed, truly enjoying this man's company. "You really have no idea how to count. How are you in a band? Don't you have to count the beats? Or measures or something?"

"Drummers count," he said. "I just feel the rhythm." He swayed and danced in his seat, and Riley burst out laughing again.

"And you need dancing lessons."

"Do you know a good teacher?" He looked at her again, his voice dropping a couple of decibels. "Maybe...*you* could be my dancing teacher."

He knew exactly how to flirt in a fun way. And how to take things more serious. And how to show that he liked her without crossing the line. Riley had never been as intrigued by a man as she was with Evan Garfield—and she wasn't sure if that was a good thing or not.

"Sure," she said, lowering her voice too. "I can teach you how to dance."

Chapter Ten

Evan hung out a couple of paces away from Riley's car, the street lamps pooling their orange light on her as she unlocked the driver's door. He really wanted to kiss her. They'd had a great afternoon and evening together, and he couldn't wait to see her again.

"Thanks, Evan," she finally said, turning toward him. "I had fun tonight."

"Me too." He smiled at her, sensing his opportunity fading right in front of him. "When can I see you again?"

"How about I text you?" she asked.

"Oh, I don't like that," he said, taking a step toward her. He put one hand on the top of the sedan behind her and inched closer. "Tomorrow night?" He brushed his lips along the side of her face, dangerously close to her ear.

"I want to see the house," she said. "You said we'd do that, and we didn't have time."

"Someone ordered too many rounds of chocolate cake," he whispered, his blood flowing like fast-moving lava in his veins.

She put gentle pressure on his chest, but Evan knew the signal. *Not tonight, rockstar.* "Tomorrow night. I'll come to your place. You show me around, cook me dinner. If you have a pool, we can swim."

"I have a pool." And now his fantasies were skipping through what her swimwear might look like.

"Call me babe again, and I won't come." She wore a very serious look on her face, and Evan knew enough not to laugh.

"I apologize that that particular endearment annoys you so much."

She nodded, still quite somber. He wasn't sure what to make of it, and he backed up another couple of feet. "And I want to know something real about you," she said.

"I've told you real things," he said, suddenly stung.

"I know." She sighed. "It just feels…does this feel real to you?"

"Yes," he said immediately. "It doesn't feel real to you?" What was he doing here, renting a house for six months and putting down roots, if it wasn't real?

"It…does," she said. "I like flirting with you. But I want serious conversation tomorrow night."

"Serious conversation," he repeated. "I can do that."

"I hope so, Evan." She tiptoed her fingers up his chest, lighting a fire with every touch, even through the fabric of his shirt. "I sure do like you, but I'm too old for games."

"Honey, I'm way older than you. I don't have time for games." And he absolutely meant that. And apparently, he could use *honey* and *sweetheart*. But not *babe*.

"You are *several* years older than me," she said with a smirk. She opened her car door and slid behind the wheel. He backed up again, waving to her as she backed out of the spot and headed for the parking lot exit.

He wasn't sure why she got to be flirty and playful when she wanted to be, and he had to be serious when she wanted him to be. How would he even know which one he was supposed to be, and when?

He frowned at the thoughts.

He could only be himself. He liked to have fun, and sing loudly in the shower, and ride fast motorcycles. He loved burgers and ice cream and a sky full of stars. The beginnings of a song started playing in his head, and he straddled his bike to get back to his new house.

The car he'd used to get to Riley's office wasn't there anymore, which meant Carl had come to get it, just as he'd said he would. Of course he had. Carl always came through for Evan.

When he got back to the house, he snapped a picture of the front door and porch from his vantage point down the front steps. It looked like it belonged in a fairy tale, what with all the yellow lights making it seem like a magical place to sleep.

But he was just a man, and it was just a house. Riley

sent him an emoji of a smiley face with hearts for eyes, so she obviously liked the house. The real question was whether she liked him.

No, that wasn't the real question. He knew she liked him. She just didn't think he was for real. So he'd show her that he was just a man, and he did normal things like other men. She wanted dinner and a lazy evening by the pool.

He didn't cook, but he knew how to order food better than anyone. Well, maybe not better than Carl, but he wasn't going to involve his brother in his romantic date.

Inside the house, with the door closed and locked behind him, a sense of privacy and security flowed over him. Carl hadn't waited up, which actually surprised Evan. He wasn't anywhere near ready for bed yet, so he stepped into the kitchen to find his brother's paperwork neatly stacked in three piles on the dining room table.

What kind of food do you like? he texted to Riley. She didn't answer for several minutes, and Evan's mind revolved around where she lived on the island. She was probably driving, and Riley was nothing if not the type of woman to ignore her phone while behind the wheel.

There's a grill here. We can have barbecue. Or burgers. Hot dogs.

Or I can get pizza.

Sushi.

I know! Chinese food. With some of those shaved ice I've heard about.

Evan just kept texting her, trying to decide if he was being serious or not. *I love all kinds of food.*

I'm sure you do, Riley finally answered. *Some of us have to watch what we eat.*

The only reason I can eat like I do is because I have a physical trainer, he tapped out to her. *It's actually in my contract.*

You have a contract that requires you to work out?

Yes, he said.

And how do you feel about that?

He thought of the picture of him in the island newspaper he'd seen on the table at her office today, and that was when he appreciated the work Jake made him do. All other times, though, he wished he could sleep in or chill out instead of working out.

It's okay, he messaged.

I sense some hesitation with that.

Who likes being yelled at while they run? He chuckled to himself. *Because if you do, I'm not sure we should see each other again.* He grinned as he imagined her laugh, glad when she sent another laughing emoji.

I don't run, she said. *You can get just as much benefit from walking.*

Do you wear those sexy heels while you walk? He stared at the message and then thumbed it off again. "Nope," he muttered to himself. "Not sending that."

Maybe we could walk together, he sent instead. *I pretty much don't have a job for a couple of months.*

I usually go in the evenings, Riley sent back. *After work.*

Monday after work then, he said, glad he'd get to see her

tomorrow too. And hopefully Saturday. And Sunday. And if he could get this walk on Monday night set, he'd be well on his way to having a real girlfriend.

"Hey," Carl said, startling Evan. He yelped and dropped his phone right as Riley's response came in.

"You're still up."

"Someone has to make sure you're still alive." Carl opened the fridge and pulled out a soda.

"I'm still alive," Evan said, instantly annoyed. He stooped to pick up his phone. "Riley's coming over tomorrow night."

Carl coughed and choked, cola spurting out of his mouth. He wiped himself up and asked, "Do I need to make myself scarce?"

"That would be great," Evan said. "I'm supposed to cook for her, and—"

"Oh, boy," Carl said, chuckling.

"And I'm going to give her a tour, and we'll lay by the pool."

"Sounds like something you'd do with a friend," Carl said, giving Evan a knowing look that pierced him right to the heart. He left the kitchen before Evan could come up with something to say, and he looked down at his phone.

He still had a message from Riley, and it said, *Maybe. If things go well tomorrow night.*

Evan really didn't like that message, but she'd sent another one. *It's so late, and I have to work tomorrow. I'll see you about six? Text me your address.*

Since he hadn't responded right away, she'd said, *Going to bed. I'll check my phone in the morning.*

He let his hand drop to his side, her messages ringing with a note of finality he didn't like. And with Carl's words bouncing around inside his mind, poisoning him, he left the kitchen with frustration building in his bloodstream.

Sounds like something you'd do with a friend.

The worst part? Carl wasn't wrong.

When he woke the next day, he texted Riley his address and got in the shower. He'd been up late plucking on his guitar and writing lyrics he'd probably never use. Didn't matter. He'd finally soothed his nerves and his ego enough to lay down. And he'd tired himself out enough to fall asleep. And in a couple of hours, he had a meeting with the billionaire group to deal with.

After that, he'd only have six more hours until he could see Riley again.

He realized how obsessive he sounded, and he told himself that he would not be asking her out again that night. If she wanted to see him again, she could suggest something.

He got on the treadmill, snapping a picture of himself to send to his trainer in California. Jake sent back several thumbs-up emojis, and Evan showered, dressed, and checked on the pool.

Riley had never said what she liked to eat, so he searched the Internet for the best food on the island of Getaway Bay, and then called the taco place that operated out of an old railway car.

They didn't deliver, but he could pick-up at five-thirty and get back to his house in the gated community where he lived.

Carl knocked on the door, and Evan pulled it open and stepped back so his brother could scrutinize his outfit. "How'd I do?"

"Actually really good," Carl said. "The slacks look great. Shirt is buttoned, but not to stuffily."

"I'm having some weird brunch with bankers and plantation owners," Evan said. "And I'm not even sure why."

"They wanted to meet you," Carl said. "And you're literally two concerts away from becoming a billionaire yourself. It wouldn't hurt you to have some connections."

Evan wasn't sure why he needed connections on the island of Getaway Bay unless he was planning to stop singing and live here full-time. The idea actually appealed to him, but he kept it inside his mind. No need to get Carl riled up before breakfast.

"Jasper is here," Carl said. "And he's a nice guy. Owns diamond mines. But nice."

"Great," Evan said, following Carl down the hall. "Are there other rockstars in the group?"

"No," Carl said. "A pineapple plantation owner. Former poker player. The woman who owns the largest financial something-or-other. The twins who own a cruise line. There is a banker."

"I knew it," Evan joked as they entered the main hall. A dark-haired man stood there, and he turned toward Evan at the sound of his voice.

"You must be Evan Garfield." He smiled as if he legit owned a diamond mine, but Evan got a genuine vibe from him.

"Guilty." He shook the man's hand. "And you're Jasper...." He glanced at Carl, sensing his brother's frustration with him. "Rosequist," he added quickly, the last name Carl had given him in an email coming to him suddenly.

"Guilty," Jasper said with a light laugh. "Are you ready? We can head over to the resort."

"Ready," Evan said, though he wasn't sure he wanted to go to brunch with a bunch of billionaires. He followed Jasper out the front door anyway, and by the time they got to Sweet Breeze, Evan had realized one thing about Jasper that he wished everyone would know about him.

He was just a regular guy.

Chapter Eleven

Riley left work late, which meant she arrived at Evan's several minutes past six. The looming gate before her wouldn't help her get to his house faster, but she had no choice but to press the button and wait for someone to say something.

"Georgia Panic," a man said, and Riley couldn't tell if it was Evan or his brother Carl.

"It's Riley Randall," she said.

"Hmm," the man said, and she knew it was Evan then. "I think Riley was supposed to be here fifteen minutes ago."

"Was she?" she asked, enjoying the flirting even through an intercom. Yes, she wanted real conversation with him too, but the man was *delightful* to flirt with.

"Yeah, and we didn't get any texts, so I'm just going to go about heating up these tacos until I hear from her."

She grabbed her phone and tapped out a quick

message to Evan. *I'm so sorry. I had a monster bride in the office, and I left late. I'll be there soon.*

Then she reached out the window and pressed the button again.

"Georgia Panic," Evan said again, and Riley almost started laughing.

"It's Riley Randall," she said as if he didn't know her last name.

"Ah, Riley. Come on in. I'll get the tacos hot." The gate started to rumble open in front of her. She eased her car through, marveling at the mansions on this part of the island. She'd worked with a lot of wealthy families and brides over the years, and she had enough money for her needs and most of her wants. But money like this… she couldn't even fathom it.

And Evan had it.

She muttered the number on his house and looked left and then right. "This way." She swung her car to the left and inched down the road, taking several long seconds just to pass one house. Er, mansion.

Finally pulling into the appointed one, she found Evan standing on that same porch he'd texted her a picture of last night, looking fresh from the shower and utterly devastating in a pair of khaki shorts and a blue button-up shirt that seemed a little tight around the biceps.

Whether he had a personal trainer yelling at him or not, the man had spent some time in a gym to his benefit.

He lifted his hand in a casual wave and put his hands in his pockets, watching her.

Riley got out of the car, stepping to the back door to get her beach bag out too. She still wore her work clothes, and navigating the dozen or so steps up to where he waited for her was going to be tricky. Especially in these heels.

Still, she found her balance with the extra weight of her bag and started the journey. Evan met her after she'd only taken three steps and said, "Let me take that bag for you." His voice sounded like melted butter and honey, and Riley paused to look up at him.

He started to take her bag, but something happened in the transfer, and it ended up on the ground. Riley didn't even care. She gazed at this man, noting that his lips curved upward because she couldn't look anywhere else.

"Hey," she said, somewhat breathlessly.

"I can't cook," he said out of nowhere. "So I know you said you wanted me to cook you dinner, but I almost started this house on fire about an hour ago." He chuckled and glanced toward the front door. "Carl actually banned me from turning on the stove again."

Riley started laughing, and she couldn't stop. Evan joined her, and she leaned into his embrace as they laughed and laughed. When she finally sobered, she asked, "So what are we eating?"

"I ordered tacos," he said. "Carl went to get them for us."

Her eyes dropped to his mouth again. "So we're alone."

"For a few minutes." He bent to pick up her bag. "Did you like how real I was there? How serious? I totally told you how flawed I am." He kicked a smile in her direction and started up the steps. He went slow, giving her a hand to hold should she need it.

She made it to the top of the steps and turned to look out toward the edge of the island. Another house sat across the street from Evan, but it was down lower, and she could see the glinting, blue water past the roof. "Wow. Great view."

"Yeah," he said, and she turned to catch him staring right at her. Without apologizing or clearing his throat or any awkwardness at all, he turned to open the front door. "Are you wearing that to sit by the pool?"

"Nope," she said. "I brought two bathing suits, actually." Why had she told him that? She didn't want to confess about her inability to make a decision quite so soon in this relationship. Sure, at work, she knew exactly what to do. Where to put a file, how to make a phone call, when to hitch on a smile and when to act surprised.

But with a famous, handsome, rich rockstar? She had no idea what she was doing. Her mind continued to add characteristics to Evan's list—kind, funny, mysterious, smart—as she followed him into the house.

She paused and looked up, taking in the grandeur of the entryway, the carved steps that went up, the huge doorways that went out. "Fancy," she said.

"It gets the job done," Evan said.

"Is the whole band staying here?" she asked, soaking in the richness of the marble beneath her feet, the dark wood on the arches in the doorways.

"Just me, Carl, and Hank," he said. "DJ went back to his hometown until we start to record again. Peter and Dan went on a cruise or something with their wives and kids. Brett went to visit my parents." He held up her bag. "Do you want to change now?"

"Yes," she said, gratefully kicking off her heels. "Will the band come back for the wedding?"

"No," he said. "I'm just singing solo."

"Oh, you do solo stuff?"

"For close friends," he said with a fast smile. So fast, she wasn't even sure she'd seen it. Riley took her bag from him, and he pointed her into a bathroom that was as big as her master suite. Everything seemed polished and high-end, and she hurried to dig through her bag, still undecided about which suit she should wear.

In September, in the evening, she wouldn't necessarily be hot. So she didn't really need to wear a two-piece. Her one-piece was almost two pieces the neckline swooped so low. She liked that it was black and hid some of the bulges surely all thirty-five-year-olds had. The two-piece was bright red, and it screamed at men to look at her.

Evan was already looking.

She shimmied into the black one-piece and pulled her coverup over her head. It was really just a big, see-through T-shirt that wafted around her body like spiderwebs. Satisfied with how she looked, she exited the bathroom to hear Evan singing across the foyer. Going that way, she found him in the kitchen putting cans of soda on the counter, his voice so full and so beautiful.

"You're a great singer," she said, causing him to cut off in the middle of a word.

"Thank you," he said. He seemed frozen to the spot and he looked down to her feet and back to her eyes several times. "You look great."

"I'm kind of tone deaf," she said. "Is that a deal-breaker for you?"

"Why would that be a deal-breaker?" He came around the island and swept one arm around her effortlessly. Riley enjoyed his warmth, his strength, the spirit she could feel oozing off of him.

"I don't know," she said. "I just wondered."

"I can't see why that would matter," he whispered, dropping his head to skate his lips across her cheek. "I'm the one who has to bring home the money with my voice."

"Mm." She held onto his shoulders and swayed with him as he pressed his lips to her neck, sliding his mouth up to her ear.

"Carl will be back soon," he said.

"Better kiss me quick then," Riley murmured.

Evan twitched, paused, and asked, "Really?"

"Are you going to make me ask twice?" She pulled back and looked up into his face.

"I'm just surprised. Last night, you...acted like I was playing with you."

Indecision raged within Riley. "I don't know what I'm doing," she admitted.

"That makes two of us," he said. "Despite what the tabloids say, I'm not super experienced with women."

"I am surprised by that," Riley said, enjoying this serious side of him.

"What about you?" he asked. "Loads of men, I assume?"

"Why would you assume that?"

"Uh, because you're drop-dead gorgeous. Smart. Funny. Talented." He pressed one finger into her back with each item he listed. "Have you been married before?"

"No," she said.

"Surprising," he said.

She didn't see how that was surprising at all. "I haven't had a whole lot of luck with men," she said, deciding to state it bluntly. "I think I'm fun. I know how to flirt. I go out with someone a few times, and everything fizzles. They don't call back." She swallowed, wondering how she'd gone from telling him to kiss her to spilling her guts about her awful dating history.

"You are fun," he said. "You do know how to flirt. And we've been out a few times already."

"Have we?"

"I think we've established that I can't count." He

grinned at her, but the gesture faded quickly. "But Riley, I'm going to call back. Again and again."

"Yeah?"

"Yeah." He leaned down then, and Riley let her eyes drift closed. She held very still, all of her nerves at attention until he touched his lips to hers. Riley's heartbeat rippled and sparks popped across her shoulders.

Evan growled in the back of his throat, kneaded her closer, and *kissed* her like she'd never been kissed before. She became hungry for him, and she couldn't get close enough to him. She kissed him back, hoping he could feel the same passion in her touch that she felt in his.

"Hey," someone said loudly, and Riley had the wherewithal to jump away from Evan. His brother stood there holding an aluminum tray of tacos. "Food's here." He glared at Evan, who ran one hand up the back of his neck, mussing up his hair.

"Hey, Carl," he said. "This is Riley Randall." He indicated her, as if Carl hadn't just seen them making out.

"Hey, Carl," she said, putting on her business skin for just a moment. "It's good to see you again." She glanced at Evan, somehow trying to communicate to him that she'd met his brother before.

At the moment, Carl didn't look like anything was nice. Not kittens, or puppies, or meeting her. He shook her hand anyway and said, "And you. Evan talks about you *constantly*."

"Hey," Evan said, but Riley secretly liked that he'd

told his brother about her. "Thanks for getting the tacos, man. I owe you one."

"Two," Carl said, leaning closer to his brother. But he didn't even attempt to speak in a lower tone when he said, "You promised me you wouldn't kiss her."

Confusion ran through Riley. Evan was forty-two-years-old. He could kiss anyone he wanted. Couldn't he?

Chapter Twelve

"She kissed me," Evan said, shooting a look at Riley. He reached for her hand and towed her around the island to where Carl had set the tacos. "Let's get something to eat. I'm starving." He took the lid off the aluminum tray to expose tortillas, beef, pico de gallo, sour cream, guacamole, black beans, and Spanish rice. Evan's stomach growled, as he hadn't eaten since the billionaire brunch that morning. He couldn't wait to tell Riley some of the stories from that meeting-slash-meal.

Carl left the kitchen, his footsteps quite loud on the stairs as he went up. Evan didn't care. Carl wasn't the boss of him, and he couldn't dictate who Evan saw or liked or kissed.

Riley glanced out the doorway, and Evan braced himself for the questions. "You promised him you wouldn't kiss me?"

"Tonight," Evan clarified. "I was, I don't know.

Putting the ball in your court." He cut a look at her out of the corner of his eye, but he couldn't get a read on her with such a short look. "I feel like I've maybe come on too strong, and I didn't want to freak you out."

"Well." She picked up a corn tortilla and spooned some sour cream onto it. "You did say you were going to call me and call me and call me. Almost sounded like a stalker."

Evan scoffed, half a laugh in the sound somewhere. "I see what you mean. That wasn't as romantic as I was hoping it would be." Though, saying he wouldn't give up on calling her was romantic for a song. He filed the lyrics away, hoping he'd remember to write them down later. He didn't have to write things down immediately when they came to him. If the lyrics were good, he'd remember them. If not...well, he didn't need lyrics even he couldn't remember. Then no one would remember them.

Riley put her hand on his, and both of them stilled. "It was actually really romantic." She looked up at him, sending Evan's pulse crashing around his ribcage again. "I'm serious when I say most men stop calling after a couple of dates."

"I really can't imagine that," he said as genuinely as possible. "I meant everything I said earlier."

"I know you did." She gave him a small smile, and they went back to assembling their food. "So." She exhaled as she reached for a brown paper bag Evan hadn't even seen his brother bring in. He wasn't sure how long Carl had stood there and watched him kiss Riley, either. He'd probably spoken to him once or twice before Riley had jumped out of his arms.

"So," he said as she took the chips and salsa over to the dining room table, along with her plate of tacos. He followed her and sat right across from her at the table.

"I'm not a brunette," she said, her green eyes dancing with mischief.

"Oh, I see what tonight is. Confessional." He bit into one of his tacos, glad they could talk about serious things and still tease.

"That's right," she said. "After my last break-up, I decided to go for a new look."

"What color is your hair?" he asked.

"Red," she said. "Sometimes I brighten up the blondes in it, and sometimes I don't. So it goes from auburn to like, shockingly red sometimes."

He tilted his head, trying to see her with red hair instead of the gorgeous mane of dark hair she currently sported. "I can't see it."

"And this isn't my real hair. Well, some of it is. But I have extensions."

Didn't matter to Evan. He wanted to fist her hair in his fingers while he kissed her again. And again. So he simply nodded and took another bite of his taco.

"Okay," she said with a big sigh. "What about you?" She dipped a chip and popped it into her mouth.

"What about me?" he asked.

"Oh, come on. I just told you a lot of stuff. How guys

dump me all the time. So much that I changed how I looked. You've got to have *some*thing."

Evan had something. He just wasn't sure he wanted it on the table right now. But Riley was wearing that sexy swimming suit, and she *had* just shared some very vulnerable things with him.

"I actually have been married," he said slowly, gauging her reaction. Anyone could read about his life online. Had she?

Those pretty eyes widened, and he had his answer. "Married? Wow."

"I mean, I'm forty-two. I have some history."

"Of course you do."

"Her name was Kitty. I'm the most embarrassed about that."

Riley snorted, the sound dying quickly. But her eyes danced with amusement, and Evan shrugged. "We were only married for a couple of years. I was thirty. I've been single for twelve years now."

"Any kids?" Riley asked, lifting her last bite of taco to her mouth.

"Nope," he said. Thank goodness. He couldn't imagine what Kitty would demand if they'd had kids together. As it was, he paid her plenty of money every month in alimony. She had traveled with him, supported him, and he'd paid for everything. But he only had to do it until she turned forty, and her birthday was coming up.

"Any serious relationships since Kitty?" Riley kept her

face angled away from Evan, and he found her absolutely adorable.

"Not really serious," he said. "I've been out with a few women, of course."

"Let me guess," she said. "You went out with them 'a few' times and stopped calling."

Shock moved right through Evan's whole system. "I travel a lot," he said, hearing the excuse in his voice. He kicked himself the moment the words left his mouth, because yes, he did travel a lot.

Riley didn't.

Why had he vocalized his temporary status on the island?

Riley was smart; surely she'd heard what he'd said, but she didn't flinch. Just finished her chips and salsa while he wolfed down another taco.

"You want the tour now?" he asked, picking up her plate with his.

"Yep," she said. "And then you need to change into your swimming trunks."

Evan smiled to himself as he put their dishes in the sink. "I'm not sure I own swimming trunks."

"Are you kidding me right now?"

He turned at the same time Riley strode toward him, pushing one palm against his chest. He started laughing and grabbed her wrist. "I'm not kidding."

"You were wearing swimming trunks the other day," she said. "When you showed up at my office unannounced?"

"Unannounced?" Evan made his voice as surprised as possible, while still chuckling. "I called first." He pulled her tight against him, despite her struggles to get away. She started laughing too and gave up trying to get away from him.

Good thing too, because Evan wanted to kiss her again. He did, their smiles quickly matching up as she met him stroke for stroke. Heat built in his body, especially when Riley's fingernails moved into his hair.

When he realized how out of control he felt, he pulled away, his breathing ragged and his heartbeat sprinting in his chest like he'd just ridden the lift up to the stage, and he could hear the crowd screaming behind him. They couldn't see him. He couldn't see them. The lights were moments away from turning on….

What a rush.

Kissing Riley was better. A thousand times better.

"Okay," he said, pulling in the deepest breath he could. "This is the kitchen and dining room. There's a mudroom over here." He walked further into the kitchen to show her the mudroom. His motorcycle boots sat there. "Garage out there," he said. "And there's an outdoor shower this way."

"An outdoor shower?" she asked. Her hand in his was so comfortable, and Evan turned to open the door opposite of the mudroom.

"Yeah," he said. "The pool is out here too, so the shower is around the corner here." He showed it to her. "Pool this way." They walked around the edge of the house, the sky above them a glorious shade of gold and crimson that took his breath away.

He stepped through the gate to the pool deck, and Riley sucked in a breath. "This is a great pool."

Evan had a pool at every house he owned, but he knew enough to keep his mouth shut about that. "I like it too," he said. "We can go back into the house from here too." He showed her the indoor shower room off the pool, which connected to the foyer.

"My bedroom is down there," he said, pointing past the shower room to the back corner of the house.

"Okay, so go change," she said.

"Right now?"

"That's right." She pressed both hands against his chest. "I want to swim, and you're not ready."

"I thought you wanted a tour of the house."

"I've seen what I want to see," she said.

Evan wasn't going to argue with her. If she wanted him to change so they could kiss in the swimming pool, he'd do it. He really didn't own any swimming trunks, but he'd been distracted from telling Riley that he'd borrowed Brett's that day on the beach. Didn't matter now, and he changed quickly and returned to the foyer.

Riley wasn't waiting for him there, but he found her standing in the formal living room, looking at a picture of his family. "Did the house come furnished?" she asked.

"Mostly," he said, looking down at the one thing he took with him everywhere. On every trip. Every tour. He pulled the picture out and set it on every desk in every hotel where he stayed. And now it was here.

"You were a cute kid," she said, smiling up at him.

"That's my mom, Chris," he said. "And my dad, Chris."

"They have the same name?"

"Yep."

Riley giggled, leaning into him as if she couldn't stand on her own. Evan really liked how she made him feel powerful, and strong, and like she needed him. He put his arm around her, because he felt like he needed her too. He hadn't known it before entering that coffee shop, but he had a Riley-shaped hole in his life that was just now getting filled.

"Where do they live?" she asked.

"Georgia," he said. "I'm from Georgia, if the band name didn't give that away."

"You don't have a very strong Southern accent."

"It comes out when I go home," he said.

"And where in Georgia is home?"

"Green Grove," he said. "My parents still live in the house where I grew up." He could still see it in his mind too, though he hadn't been back for a while. Touring was exhausting, and he thought he probably should go visit his parents at some point. Then he remembered he'd committed to Thanksgiving with them.

His first thought was to invite Riley, but he'd already made a pact with himself not to ask her out again. No way he was inviting her on a family trip during the holidays that was still two months away.

Nope. Not happening.

"It's a big house," he said. "Out in the country, near the Appalachian Mountains."

"I don't think of you as a country boy at all," she said.

"We all have a little bit of country in us," he said.

She cocked her head, finally tearing her eyes from the family photo he'd set on the piano in the formal living room. "Is that one of your songs?"

Evan laughed and tugged her away from the living room. "I don't normally quote my own lyrics, I promise."

"Yeah, let's not make that a habit," she said dryly.

"Let's go swim," he said. "The night is beautiful, and I want to see that swimming suit without that shirt covering it up."

"It's a see-through shirt," she said, rolling her eyes.

"Yeah, not quite." He led her out to the pool, carefully peeling his shirt over his head. Riley made a girly squeak, and he watched her slide her eyes up and down his body. He was suddenly grateful for every squat he'd done, chin-up he'd growled through, and mile Jake had made him run.

Chapter Thirteen

Riley sighed as she set her phone down and turned it over. Her productivity at Your Tidal Forever had fallen off a cliff. Hope hadn't noticed yet, but she would soon enough. Charlotte had already seen Riley texting longer than she should have, and she'd pulled a few files herself, made a few phone calls Riley normally did, and covered for her so she and Evan could have longer lunches together.

The man was made of cotton candy and steel, one for his lips and one for his abs. A couple of weeks had passed since swimming at his house, and every activity they did brought out a new part of him she liked.

His strength while they hiked up to the waterfalls. His laugh when she told him about her initial dye job. "I shouldn't have tried to do it myself," she'd told him while he laughed and laughed. His sense of family every time she thought about that picture. His talent when she heard him singing on the boardwalk while he waited for her to come outside and go to lunch with him.

Sometimes she hung out just inside the door, not committed to leaving just so she could hear that voice. Oh, that voice did things to her stomach that shouldn't be legal.

She saw him every day, which was odd for her. She liked time to herself too, and she didn't want to overwhelm the men she dated. But Evan didn't seem overwhelmed, and Riley found herself lonely when she wasn't with him.

September became October, and the weather cooled slightly. Hawaii was entering its rainy season, and Riley's hair didn't like the shift in climate. She spent too long straightening it in the morning, especially because it was so long. "Time for a new do," she said one morning as she stood in front of the mirror.

Pulling out her phone, she texted Tessa, her stylist. They had an appointment coming up in a couple of days, but Riley didn't want the same cut and color. *I need something new*, she typed out. *Suggestions?*

Do you want to go back to red? Tessa asked. *You're literally like, the only person I know that can pull off that look.*

Riley looked up from her phone. She wasn't sure if she wanted to go back to her red hair, light eyebrows, making her freckles stand out. Right now, she covered everything up, drew on thicker eyebrows, made her hair the color of coal.

She certainly didn't want to go back to the woman she'd been with red hair.

Maybe just something shorter, she sent to Tessa. *How do you think I'd look with a pixie cut?*

Adorable, Tessa said. *You have the perfect bone structure in your face for short hair.*

But Evan had told her how much he liked her long hair, and he ran his fingers through it while he kissed her. So she couldn't cut it all off. Maybe just enough not to have to use the extensions. That would save her time and money at the salon too.

She wandered out to the kitchen and set her coffee to brew. Her house compared to Evan's was a joke, and she'd been learning to stop comparing. She let him pay for lunches and dinners and dolphin tours. Scuba diving lessons and snorkeling day trips and petrified lightning. He had the money, and he liked spending it on her.

She'd learned he was paying Kitty alimony for a few more months. He'd told her about his time in college, and how Georgia Panic came to be a band. She knew what flavor of ice cream he always ordered, and she knew he'd never put anything coconut-flavored in his mouth.

In some moments, when it was very quiet, she still didn't believe that he liked her. Such a thing seemed impossible, but he kept calling, kept showing up, and kept kissing her like he liked her. More than that—like he was falling in love with her.

The very idea scared her to death, and she sighed as

she bent to pick up Sunshine, who'd been rubbing around her ankles for several seconds now. "Where's Marbles, huh? Isn't he hungry this morning?"

The gray cat would come as soon as Riley used the can opener. Marbles was picky, and he only liked wet cat food while Sunshine preferred dry. Riley did what the cats wanted, and she washed out their bowls and got them fresh water and food.

Sure enough, when the can opener whirred, Marbles came running from outside, the flap of the cat door making a slapping noise as he jumped through it. "There you go, Marbles," she said, stroking her hand down the cat's back. He purred and went right to work on eating his food, Sunshine beside him as she crunched her way through her breakfast.

Riley's thoughts returned to Evan, as they'd started doing more and more often. She needed to learn to compartmentalize, but admittedly, she wasn't great at it.

Her phone buzzed, and she glanced down at it. *I can look through some things today*, Tessa had said. *Text you some pictures.*

That would be great, thanks. Riley put her phone in her pocket then, grabbed a water bottle from the fridge, and put two granola bars in her purse. After doctoring up her coffee with cream and sugar the way she liked, she set off for work.

She had to focus at work today. She simply had to. If she could get caught up on the filing and get her phone calls done, she could enjoy lunch. After that, she was sitting in on two meetings with new consultants, one of her favorite parts of her job—training them to be more organized in what they did.

If the consultants did a good job, Riley's job was much easier too. And she loved getting to know new people, and both of the wedding planners Hope had just hired were great.

Once at Your Tidal Forever, she stopped by Lisa's office to see how her friend's latest date had gone. She hadn't texted last night, which could mean anything. The date could've been spectacular, and Lisa had been out really late. Too late to text. Or the date could've been terrible, and Lisa was embarrassed to text.

She looked up as Riley's heels clicked into her office. "I didn't text you."

"I know that," Riley said, cocking one hip and taking the last sip of her almost cold coffee. "That's why I'm here right now."

A smile bloomed on Lisa's face, and Riley couldn't help grinning back. "You like him, don't you?"

"Yes," Lisa said. "But I don't want to jinx it."

"Who is he?"

"I'm not saying yet."

"Did you meet him on the app?"

"Surprisingly, no." Lisa stood up and picked up two folders. "Now, go get to work." She handed the folders to Riley. "I don't pepper you with questions about your world-famous Sexiest Boyfriend Alive."

Riley scoffed as she took the folders. "Uh, yes, you

do." Or at least she had. "You made me call you in the middle of the night once."

"That was because you said you were going to a very risky part of the island at night," Lisa said, flipping her long, blonde hair over her shoulder. "*Some*one had to make sure you got home safe."

"Yeah, Evan did that."

"I bet he did," Lisa said, settling at her desk again. She looked up at Riley, who was silently begging her to tell who she'd gone out with twice now. Twice, and she was still excited about him. "I'm not saying anything else."

"Fine," Riley said, though she wasn't really mad. "But I bet you fifty bucks I figure it out before you tell me."

"That's not fair," Lisa called after her as Riley left the office. "You have ways of knowing who I call!"

Riley giggled to herself, because she did have access to the phone records of everyone at Your Tidal Forever. And since they got cell phones for work, hardly anyone paid for a personal phone. They just used their work one, which meant Lisa had been texting and calling this guy from her work phone, and Riley would be able to figure out who it was.

She wouldn't though, at least not right away. She loved and respected Lisa, and if she wasn't ready to tell who her mystery guy was yet, she wasn't ready. That was okay.

Riley sat behind her desk, a sigh already leaking from

her mouth. She filed Lisa's folders and opened her computer. She loved lists and keeping track of what needed to be done, and she'd already made a list for today. Your Tidal Forever didn't open officially until ten, which meant she had a couple of hours to catch up on things before the phone started ringing.

The front door of the building opened, causing a bell to chime. Riley looked up, half-expecting to see Evan there. Instead, she found Ash Lawson, the best dressmaker on the island.

"Hey, Ash," she said. "Who do you need?"

"Betty," she said, lugging her huge suitcase full of fabrics and dress samples. "I'll just go back."

"All right," Riley said, picking up her phone anyway. Three digits later, she said, "Betty, Ash is coming back."

"Thanks, Riley," Betty said, and Riley returned her attention to the to-do list typed on her computer.

She bent her head and got some tasks done, knowing Evan would show up sooner or later, and she'd still have a list a mile long. The door chimed sometime later, and she looked up, trained as she was to that bell.

Her sexy rockstar entered, and she couldn't help the sigh and giggle that came from her mouth. But Evan didn't look happy. "Hey," she said, standing. "What's up? Is it lunchtime already?"

"It's past lunchtime." He frowned. "I texted you that I couldn't go to lunch, but I'd stop by later. You responded."

Had she? Confused, she looked down at her phone.

Sure enough, the clock said it was almost three. As if spurred by the time realization, her stomach growled. She hadn't even pulled out one of her emergency granola bars.

"Oh, right." She didn't check his texts. If he said she'd responded, she probably had. "What's up?"

"I have to go to California tomorrow."

Pure shock hit her like icy water. She lost her breath for a moment, her chest automatically seizing before it released. "Oh."

"It's just for a week or two," he said. "We're meeting with our agent about some stuff." He never got too technical with her when it came to band business. The terms he used were always "stuff" and "things" and "whatever else Carl wants me to do."

"All right," she said, because how could she keep him from doing his job? He'd mentioned once that he could do video calls, even while the band wrote music, something Georgia Panic did together, apparently. Usually in Evan's Malibu home, but sometimes in Hank's house that was further inland, or DJ's mansion overlooking the ocean.

All the members in Georgia Panic had homes in California.

"I'm sorry," Evan said. "I know we were going on that three-hour cruise."

"It's fine," Riley said. "They let you cancel the tickets for a full refund." And if they didn't, Evan wouldn't miss fifty bucks. Plus, maybe they then wouldn't get shipwrecked and stuck on an outlying island for years.

"I'm packing tonight," he said. "But you could come hang out?"

Riley liked that he'd invited her, but she suddenly didn't want to go. She didn't want to watch him pack and walk out of her life. She felt like she'd gotten on a roller coaster she didn't know would have such sharp turns, and her stomach swooped from side to side, disorienting her.

She put her hands flat against the desktop in front of her. "Maybe," she said.

"Maybe?" Evan's eyebrows went up.

"I'll just be in the way," she said. "I've been meaning to go get a new skirt. Maybe I'll just go do that. I'll see you when you get back." She really wanted him to come back. But the truth was, he didn't have anything tying him to Getaway Bay.

Anything but her, that was.

And she wasn't sure she was a strong enough draw for a man like Evan Garfield.

"Riley," he said, that voice she loved low and somewhat dangerous. "This isn't permanent, you know. I'm coming back."

"I know," she said.

"You have that panicked look in your eyes."

"It's just sudden," she said. "I'm working through it still." He had no return date, so how was she supposed to feel?

"I'd ask you to come with me, but I know you'd say

no," he said, stepping around the counter and taking her into his arms. If Hope came out and saw them, she wouldn't like it, but Riley melted into Evan's embrace anyway.

"Come tonight," he said gently. "Even just to kiss me goodbye. I'm leaving at six-thirty in the morning."

She couldn't refuse him when he held her so intimately and spoke so genuinely. So she said, "Okay, I'll see you later tonight," and hoped she hadn't just given him her whole heart to fly away with.

Chapter Fourteen

Evan heard the blasted grandfather clock downstairs start to sing, and annoyance rang through him. He couldn't help counting the chimes, and while Riley had teased him about not being able to count, he certainly could in that moment.

Nine. Nine chimes.

And Riley still hadn't shown up.

"She said she'd come," Evan said, looking into his full suitcase. He'd finished his laundry and packing about five minutes ago, but he couldn't face going out into the rest of the house alone. Carl was surely sitting at the kitchen table, their flight itineraries printed in front of him, though Evan had everything he needed on his phone.

He'd been telling himself for two hours not to text her. But she'd probably be upset he hadn't. Evan wasn't sure how to win with Riley, and he really wanted to.

So he picked up his phone and tapped out a quick

message to her. *Finished packing. Want to grab a shaved ice or something?*

Aren't you leaving early in the morning? The speed with which her text came in after his brought him little comfort.

I'll sleep when I'm dead, he said. *Tell me where you are, and I'll come pick you up.* His text was fairly demanding, and he erased the last sentence.

Instead of getting another text from Riley, he got a phone call. Surprise moved through him, rendering him a little slow to answer the call. "Hey," she said. "I've been outside in my car for oh, I don't know. A while."

Evan was already moving toward his bedroom door. "You have? Why didn't you come in?"

"I don't know."

Evan went past the stairs and to the front door, pulling it open as if he'd rip it off the hinges. A few more steps, and he stood on the edge of the porch, Riley's car in sight. She got out and hung up the phone at the same time.

Their eyes met across the distance, and Evan pocketed his phone and jaunted down the steps to meet her. "There you are." he said, a little surprised at how relieved he was that she'd come. She wore that same edge of panic in her eyes now as she had hours ago.

"Sorry," she said, running her hand through her hair. "I just…I don't know. I don't want to tell you to go, but I'm not happy you're going."

"It's just a work thing," he said, trying to understand her perspective.

Riley stepped into his arms and held onto him. They just breathed together, and Evan didn't want to scare her away or ruin the moment. But he couldn't help saying, "Help me understand."

"I…it's just that I know you're not permanent here, and I was kind of hoping you would be."

"No matter where I live, I'm always going to travel," he said as gently as he could. "That's what a band does, Riley."

She nodded and stepped back, pulling her T-shirt down. "I know. But you just finished a tour, right?"

"Right."

"And it'll be a couple of years before you have another one." She looked at him with so much hope in those green eyes.

"Probably," he said. "But we get asked to do stuff all the time. Play at awards shows. Concerts for charities. Fireworks shows." He could go on and on. And Georgia Panic always took the gigs they got offered. They hadn't been featured at the Superbowl yet, and that was on Evan's bucket list.

"Are you trying to get me to break up with you?" she asked.

"No," he said simply. "Can we play this by ear? I'm just going to LA for a few meetings. I'll be back before you know it."

"Sure," Riley said in a semi-false tone. He knew she

didn't want to play anything by ear. And that he wouldn't be back before she knew it. But Evan wasn't sure what else he could say or do. He'd been a member of Georgia Panic for two decades, and this was his life.

DJ had a girlfriend who just traveled everywhere with him. Maybe Riley could do that. She was great with people and paperwork, and she could be the band's public relations manager. Or she could just be with him.

"Okay." Evan said, trying to get his thoughts to align. "So is that a no to the shaved ice?"

Riley giggled, and Evan hoped it was the beginning of her softening up a little bit. Relaxing. He wished she knew she didn't need to have everything worked out right now.

"I'll take a shaved ice," she said. "And I know just the place. Have you been to that rainbow place?"

"Not unless you've taken me there, sweetheart," he said. "I don't do a whole lot without you."

She scoffed and took her hand in his. "Yeah, right. I'll drive, because I don't feel like flirting with death tonight."

Evan shook his head, his smile coming easily. "All right. Take me to the rainbow snow. I'm parched."

She drove, and the conversation between them focused on her job and his songwriting. She didn't ask him what he'd be doing in Los Angeles, and he didn't tell her when he'd be back. They enjoyed their sweet treat as the sun went down, and when Riley dropped him off back at his house, he took her fully into his arms and kissed her.

"I'll call you tomorrow when I get there, okay?"

"Okay," she said, touching her mouth to his once more. Evan went up the stairs and into the house, the tingling sensation in his lips a sure reason that he'd be returning to Getaway Bay. Riley Randall had turned his life upside down with an email about his watch, and he was so glad he'd lost that timepiece.

"WAIT, WAIT, WAIT," HE SAID INTO HIS PHONE AS HE walked off the plane. "You're talking way too fast, DJ. Start again. They want what?" Evan could feel people staring at him, recognizing him, but he didn't care. He mashed his ball cap lower over his eyes and got out of the stream of traffic as DJ started talking again.

"They want us to sign a deal where we only release singles," he said, much slower this time and with far fewer curse words. "No album, Evan."

"No album?" Those words didn't make sense. "But we've been with them for twelve years, and our last album went double platinum."

"It's a new model, John says."

Evan didn't care what John said. "I can't believe TriCities doesn't want an album. We were their number one selling album last year." Georgia Panic had won the People's Choice Award, for crying out loud. They sold out stadiums from coast to coast.

And their record label didn't want another album?

"I know." DJ exhaled heavily on the other end of the line. "They want us to write the standard album set. Name it. Name the songs. But they don't want to release them as an album. They want to try a dozen singles, spread out every three or four weeks."

"This makes no sense," Evan said, watching a man walk by with a pretty redhead at his side. He thought about Riley, and what she might look like with red hair. "We'd be releasing for a year."

"Right? It sounds like a stupid plan."

"Well, we'll sit down and talk to Greg. See what he has to say."

"There should be a car for you there at the airport," DJ said. "Get here fast, would you? I feel like there are sharks circling."

The call ended, but Evan didn't move away from the wall. "Sharks," he repeated to himself. *Great.*

Not that the band hadn't dealt with people trying to take advantage of them in the past. But Evan just wasn't feeling up to the task today. He mourned the loss of the Hawaii beach he'd just left—and the woman he'd met there.

Pull yourself together, he told himself as he finally joined the fray of people streaming toward the baggage claim area. *Riley will be there when you get back.*

He hadn't left permanently, and while it took a long time to fly to Getaway Bay and back, he could do it.

"Everything okay?" Carl asked, and Evan cut a glance at him.

"I guess we'll see." They found their driver and collected their bags before heading for downtown LA. Carl kept his eyes glued to his phone as the car maneuvered closer and closer to a tall office building where the agent for the band, Greg Stone, worked.

Evan had been in Greg's office dozens of times, including when the band had signed one of the most lucrative deals in the music industry. John Feehan at TriCities Records had secured cool digital artists for their album covers, and since making the move to TriCities and away from Lionshead, Georgia Panic's popularity and income had swelled and swelled and swelled.

Evan was on the brink of becoming a billionaire, and apparently the rich and powerful men and women on the island of Getaway Bay knew that. He shook the billionaire brunch he'd attended on the island out of his head. He couldn't be thinking about things hundreds of miles away.

He needed his focus here, now. The car pulled up to the building and Carl got out first. Evan didn't travel with security, though his brother wanted him to. He said, "All right," and Evan got out too. They went into the building together and Carl gave their names to the guard at the front desk.

He cleared them through to the elevators, where they went up to the sixteenth floor. Greg was part of a larger talent agency, but Syd still sat at the front desk.

"Carl," she said, a smile brightening her face. "Evan.

Greg is expecting you. Can I get you something to drink?"

"Yes, please," Carl said, shooting the brunette a smile. She hurried off to fetch water, and Carl watched her go. Evan smothered a smile as he stepped over to the fish tank against the wall. *Sharks circling* ran through his mind, but there were no sharks in this tank.

"Here you go," Syd said, handing them each a bottle of water.

"Thanks," they said in unison, and then Evan started past Syd's desk. The sooner they could get to a room where the door closed, the better.

DJ, Hank, Dan, and Peter were already there. Brett was in Georgia, and he hadn't made the trip today. Carl had assured Evan that Brett would be in town tomorrow.

"Hey, guys," Evan said, a complete sense of belonging flowing over him. These were his bandmates. His best friends. Whatever Greg said, they could weather.

"Greg," he said, shaking his agent's hand. "I hope I'm not too late. I took the first flight off the island."

"Not too late," Greg said, tugging on the end of his sleeves before he sat down. "We've gotten in a new proposal from TriCities."

Their last contract had just been fulfilled, what with the six solid months of touring, of sleeping in a trailer, of performing in front of thousands of screaming fans. Greg had told them a new contract would come as soon as the tour wrapped up, and it seemed like it had.

"They want two more albums." He smiled around at

the members of the group.

"Really?" DJ asked. "In album form?" He glanced at Evan, but just because he was the front man on stage didn't mean he led the group in everything they did.

"They do want to try a new distribution method," Greg admitted. "But I've been over the contract and over it. I gave it to my mentor for him to go over. The label wants twenty-eight songs from you, grouped into two albums, but they might release single after single until the whole album is out. Then they'll produce the album at a later date."

That was slightly different than what DJ had said on the phone. Evan felt like he was taking risks left and right. First, with his heart and Riley. Second, when he said, "Sounds great, Greg. Where do we sign?"

He counted—and reminded himself to tell Riley that he'd done so—to five, and then chaos erupted.

"Wait a second," DJ said. "You can't just decide for all of us."

"I think a new distribution model is a bad idea," Peter said.

Carl said something too, but Evan wasn't sure what because Hank was yelling and so was Dan. No one in the band looked happy, and at least now Evan knew where they all stood.

With him. They all stood with him.

Now they just needed to figure out what game TriCities was playing—and whether or not Georgia Panic wanted to join in.

Chapter Fifteen

Riley typed and filed and made phone calls. Anything to keep her mind off of Evan and how far away he was.

She didn't know what was wrong with her. She'd dated a lot of men, and she always ended up single again. Some men were easier to get over than others, of course, but she'd never been this anxious or this miserable—and Evan was just away on business.

By lunchtime, he'd texted just once. *Made it. Miss you already.*

Riley couldn't help sighing and smiling at her phone at the few simple words. The intercom on her phone beeped, and she jumped. "Riley, we need you back here," Hope said through the speaker.

"Is it time already?" Riley had been invited to the meeting about the mayor's daughter's wedding to make sure notes were taken and assignments noted so nothing got missed.

Hope didn't answer her, because yes, it was time already. Five minutes past time. Riley practically pushed her chair back into the wall behind the counter where she worked, grabbed her notebook, and hurried down the hall to Hope's office.

She'd been working at Your Tidal Forever for years, but Hope Sorenson still inspired some fear in her. "Sorry," she said upon entering the office and finding everyone else there. Charlotte smiled at her in the same, calm way Charlotte did everything. She wasn't the official consultant on this wedding, but Regina wanted something custom for her wedding, and Charlotte had the best brain when it came to custom altars, ceremonies, and dresses.

Lisa and Shannon were working the wedding together, and they were both settled on a loveseat, a huge binder open across their laps.

Riley took a seat on the couch where Charlotte sat and flashed a smile in Hope's direction. "Sorry," she said again.

"It's fine," Hope said, glancing away from her laptop on her desk. "Shannon?"

Shannon had been working closely with Hope to become the president of Your Tidal Forever one day, and Riley really liked her. She was much less intimidating than Hope, but her expectation for perfection was the same.

"Let's start with the venue," Shannon said. "Regina is a little bit older, and she has some very specific ideas of what she wants."

"What she *doesn't* want," Lisa said, and she and Shannon exchanged a look. Riley tried not to roll her eyes. The last thing she wanted to deal with right now was a Bridezilla with political ties.

"Right," Shannon said, flipping a few pages in their binder. "She doesn't want anything overhead obstructing the sunshine. She doesn't want anything with too many things that will 'fly away,' meaning streamers, vines, stuff like that. She doesn't want a teeny tiny altar, but something, and I quote, 'with beef.'"

Charlotte snorted, and Riley looked at her. She burst out laughing in the next moment, and Shannon giggled too.

"Beef," Charlotte said between chuckles. "I just… sorry." She quieted and looked at Hope, who was smiling. "I was just imagining like a cow-themed altar or something."

"Heft," Lisa said, giggling, and Riley found herself joining in another round of laughter. This meeting was exactly what she needed to get her spirits back up, and she hadn't even known it.

Shannon continued to read Regina's rather lengthy list of things she didn't want, and Charlotte said, "I'll come up with a few sketches we can show her. When will she be back in again?"

"Next Friday," Lisa said, glancing down. "She wants

Ash to design the dress." She looked at Riley "What's her schedule like right now?"

Riley started tapping on her phone to get to the right calendar. "I know she's booked pretty far out…." Swipe, tap, type, swipe. "It wouldn't be until January before she could start making the dress. She'd meet with Regina well before that, of course."

"Let's get on her schedule," Lisa said, making a note for herself in the binder. "I'll tell Regina about the timeline, but it should be fine. Her wedding isn't until next April."

Riley nodded and added *call Ash about Regina Keani's wedding* to her own to-do list. The meeting continued, and Riley kept detailed notes of which assignments were given to whom, and when things needed to happen. She'd put everything in the shared calendar, and everyone on the team would get notified when dates and deadlines were approaching.

A few hours later, she returned to the front desk to find a bouquet of flowers sitting there. She stopped mid-stride, and Charlotte almost hit her from behind. "Riley, what's going on?" She moved around her, bumping her as she did. "Oh. Those must be from Evan, right?" She glided over to the desk where Riley worked and plucked the card out of the dozens and dozens of red roses sitting there.

Riley's breath hitched in her throat. Maybe she'd been overreacting about Evan. Of course he was going to travel for his band. They'd talked about it already. She just needed more time to process how his life was going to go, and how it impacted hers. If she'd known about this trip for the last couple of weeks, she'd have been more prepared to go home alone tonight.

"They're from Evan, all right." Charlotte turned around, the open card in her hand. She grinned at Riley like she'd won the lottery and handed her the card on her way into her office. "You've got yourself a real charmer there, Riles."

"Thanks," Riley said, hating the nickname but not saying anything about it. She glanced down at the card.

Sorry I had to leave so suddenly. I miss you and I'll call you tonight and I can't wait to show you my house here in Malibu.

With love,

Evan

Her heart fluttered in her chest, the same way the small card did as it floated to the ground after she'd dropped it.

With love.

The phone rang, shattering the stupor she'd fallen into. She bent to pick up the card before hurrying the last few steps to her desk to answer the call. So she'd go home alone tonight. It wasn't the end of the world.

Evan was coming back.

LATER THAT NIGHT, RILEY SAT ON HER LANAI, WATCHING the sun sink into the ocean on the horizon and eating the Chinese take-out she'd picked up on the way home. Evan had texted to say he was minutes away from being home, and he'd call her as soon as he could.

But twenty minutes had gone by, and her phone hadn't made a peep. She glanced at it again just to make sure it had enough battery, and it was fully charged. Still plugged in, even.

Foolishness hit her, and she picked up another egg roll. Before she could take a bite, her phone rang. She dropped the food back into the Styrofoam container and swiped on Evan's call.

"Hey," she said.

"Hey." A huge exhale came with his voice, and he sounded tired.

"Long day?"

"So long. Did you know Hawaii is three hours behind California?"

Riley smiled. "Everyone knows that, Evan."

"Yeah, well, my old bones didn't know it." He sighed again. "I had a little trouble getting in my own house."

"Oh, this sounds like a good story," she said.

"It's embarrassing." He chuckled, and she could just imagine him lying on a fancy leather couch in his posh Malibu home, talking on the phone to her.

To *her*.

It still seemed a little bit surreal that someone like

him could like someone like her. Maybe even love her, if that card that had come with the roses was really true.

She'd been telling herself for hours that using *with love* was just how people signed cards. It was no big deal. Those words didn't actually mean that Evan was in love with her.

"You don't have to tell it if you don't want to," she said.

"I'll save it for another time," he said. "I wanted to talk to you about my meetings today."

"Oh, am I going to get to know what 'stuff' you talked about today?"

"Yeah," he said. "It was pretty ugly, number one. But the band is on the same page. Basically, our record company wants more music from us, which is great. But they don't want full albums, not really. They want songs they can release as singles over time, and then maybe, in the future, they'll box them up and sell them as an album too."

"That's...weird," Riley said, though she didn't know much about the music industry. "I've never heard of that."

"Exactly," Evan said, his voice bringing more passion with it now. "And what most people don't understand is that not every song is a single."

"Yeah, I don't know what that means," Riley said.

"It means that the songs we release early off an album, those are singles. They're our best songs. The most popular ones. The ones you hear on the radio over and over again. Not every song is catchy, popular, or played on the radio fifty times a day."

"Are your songs played on the radio fifty times a day?" she asked, teasing him.

"Ha ha," he said. "But you get the idea."

"I do," she said. "And I got the flowers too. Thank you, Evan. They're stunning."

He only hesitated for half a heartbeat before saying, "Like you, Riley," and making her smile.

"How long will you be there?" she asked, wishing he was here instead. Even with that ridiculous motorcycle. She'd climb on the back and hold him tight as they flew through the night.

"I don't know yet," he said. "I know that's not what you want to hear. But the meeting devolved very quickly today, and we've got a call with our producer at TriCities tomorrow. I might know more then."

Another man spoke to him in the background, and Evan said, "Riley, I have to go, sweetheart. I'll talk to you again soon, okay?"

"Okay," she said, wishing she didn't feel so small and insignificant compared to him. It wasn't fair to put him so high up on a pedestal, but she didn't have anyone giving her a hard time about coming into her own home or anyone there with her to remind her to take her vitamins, manage her money, or keep her schedule straight.

She couldn't judge him, though. Evan had lived his

rockstar life for twenty years, and he wasn't going to change now.

That thought stuck in the back of her throat like an errant popcorn kernel.

No, he wasn't going to change now—not even for her.

Chapter Sixteen

Evan plucked the strings on the guitar in his music room, ignoring his phone and Carl's insistence he open the door. He didn't normally throw temper tantrums, but the last eleven days in LA had been some of the most maddening of his life.

He'd held meetings right here in this room with just the core five members of Georgia Panic. No girlfriends. No wives. No kids. No managers. No brothers. Just the five of them.

He wanted to go back to Getaway Bay and the vacation he'd been promised. It didn't seem fair that he'd only gotten a couple of weeks with Riley and the beach before having to deal with his career again.

He didn't whine about it to anyone, though. After all, no one wanted to listen to a spoiled rockstar complain about having to work. And he wasn't really complaining.

He just felt the chasm between him and Riley growing with every day he stayed in Los Angeles.

And he didn't want to attend another meeting. Or take another phone call from some executive at the record label across the country. He didn't want to go to another dinner, and have another discussion.

So he'd locked himself in the music room, and he was playing and writing songs the way he wanted them. There was no pressure to make amazing singles and come up with lyrics and beats and chords no one else had heard when he was alone in the music room.

Besides, this song currently flowing from him would never make it onto any album. It was for Riley, and she would be the only one he'd sing it for. He leaned over and made a few notes on the stand in front of him, adjusting the tempo and jotting down the notes in his head.

He plucked them on the guitar next, feeling the vibrations move through him. This song was more of a ballad, like what someone might dance to. He could feel Riley in his arms, swaying with him as he started to sing.

Evan knew he had a gift for songwriting. He'd always known it. The ability had been born inside him, and he'd worked over the years to bring it out, let it flow, and capture the deepest emotions he could.

He'd paired up with other talented musicians, and he'd spent his life doing exactly what he'd always dreamed he would—sharing music with others.

Carl had stopped pounding on the door, and Evan let

the last of the music flow through him. He wrote everything down and closed the red and white striped notebook on the stand. No one ever came in here, so he left it where it was and went to leave the room.

Surprisingly, Carl wasn't standing in the hallway waiting for him, and Evan went downstairs to find his brother. He pulled his phone out of his back pocket and found dozens of texts. He skipped all of them except Brett's, who'd said he and Carl were going to the meeting and they'd simply say he wasn't feeling up to it.

Oh, and they'd bring dinner back.

"Great," Evan muttered to himself. He'd been in the music room for hours, and he didn't care about yet another meeting with yet another stuffy suit who wanted to dictate to them how and when and what kind of music Georgia Panic should make.

As he was still staring at his phone, another message came in. *You didn't go to the meeting either?*

Evan called Dan instead of texting him back. As their lead guitarist, Dan had mad skills with his fingers. He didn't say much in meetings, but Evan had learned to read his thoughts and mood on his face. He didn't like what had been happening the last several days either.

"I didn't go," Evan said. "I just couldn't. We've said what we wanted to say, you know?"

"I hear you, brother," Dan said. "DJ boycotted it too. Peter said he'd go, but Hank actually left town today. He said his kids have some fall concert they're doing, and he's not missing it for this."

"Good for him," Evan said, wondering if he could pick his bandmate's brain about maintaining a relationship and a family while being in a band. Evan had never given the topic much thought, but if things continued with Riley, he suspected he might have some juggling lessons to learn.

"Want to get dinner?" Dan asked.

"Carl and Brett went to the meeting," Evan said. "They said they'd bring dinner home." He suddenly didn't want to eat whatever they brought him and listen to them detail the meeting. "So yeah, let's go to dinner."

Dan laughed, and Evan smiled while he tried to remember where he'd stowed the keys to any of the cars or motorcycles in the ten-car garage behind the house. He couldn't even remember the last time he'd been in Malibu, which was why it had taken some convincing for the security detail to let him inside the house, despite his lack of a key.

He'd had ID though, and in the end, he'd gotten inside before Carl knew he'd misplaced his house key —again.

"Jane's?" Dan asked, and Evan agreed readily. The small restaurant was always busy, but never crowded. They could sit in a corner booth and just eat without having to fill every moment with chatter.

"See you in an hour," Evan said, and he hung up. While he lived in the house, he employed people to help out. He maintained the maid service biweekly even when he wasn't living in the house. Maybe one of them had seen his keys....

He called the service and asked, and sure enough, their supervisor said the keys had been placed in a sectioned plastic box in the top drawer next to the fridge. When Evan opened the drawer, he found each key slot labeled with the type of car or truck or bike it started.

"Perfect," he said, wishing his mind worked in such an organizational way. But it so didn't. He chose a key for a sporty convertible, as it was decently warm in LA, even though October had arrived.

As he drove down the winding roads out of the hills and toward the freeway that would take him to Jane's, he only had one thought: *I wish Riley were here with me.*

He'd contemplated a lot over the past eleven days, and one of those things was to ask her to come with him. They didn't have to get married right away. He owned a house with seven bedrooms, for crying out loud. Or she could get her own place in town. Or live in the pool house. The options really were endless.

"She won't give up her job," he told himself for the tenth time as he made the turn to get on the freeway. She wouldn't have to work at all, but Evan knew Riley well enough to know she couldn't just lie by the pool every day. A day here or there, yes. But not every day.

She liked being busy, and she was very good at her job.

"She could get a job here," he said next, because in his world, everything was so simple. But again, he knew when it came to Riley, nothing was very simple. How he felt about her was complex, and how she viewed their relationship was too.

Being separated from her had actually been good for Evan, because it had shown him that he really liked this woman as a person. Not just because she was gorgeous and fun to kiss, though she was both of those things too.

He liked talking to her on the phone, and listening to her tell stories about her co-workers, her friends, the island, her nieces and nephews. He told her things too, and it felt so nice to share his life with someone. Have a real friend.

Of course, his bandmates were friends too, but he wasn't going home to any of them at night. No, he wanted to go home to Riley at the end of every day.

"Going home," he said as the sign for Jane's came into view. "That's the name of the song." A smile danced across his face. Naming songs wasn't usually his forte, but hey, this one felt right.

He pulled into the parking lot at the same time he got a text. *You're still singing at the wedding, right?* Charlie had asked.

Of course, bro, Evan tapped out quickly. *When is it again?*

Very funny. Charlie sent an eye rolling emoji. *It's December fifteenth.*

I've got it on my calendar, Evan said. *Can't wait! Do you have any special requests? What's Amelia's favorite song?*

I'll get back to you, Charlie said, and Evan took that to

mean his friend didn't know his fiancée's favorite song. For some reason, that made him chuckle, and he wondered what Riley's was.

Dan waited on the sidewalk in front of the restaurant, but Evan took another moment to text Riley quickly.

What's your favorite song?

Then he went to meet his friend, glad he and Riley would have something to talk about later. Something that meant a lot to him—music.

Four days later, he touched down in Getaway Bay, a huge sense of relief covering him. He also knew he'd have a piper to pay once Carl found out he'd skipped town. But he was forty-two years old, and Greg could text him when the next offer came in from TriCities. He didn't need to lounge around in Malibu to get a text.

So he'd packed his bag and driven himself to the airport while Carl slept. And now he was back on the island where Riley was, fifteen days after he'd left.

He'd texted her that he was coming, and he hoped she'd be waiting for him down by the baggage claim. He didn't see her as he passed by the people going into the airport, and he didn't see her as he waited for his luggage.

Once he'd gotten his bag, he turned again, trying to find her.

"Excuse me, sir?" a woman asked, and Evan paused. He really didn't want to sign autographs right now. He just wanted to see Riley, and hold Riley, and kiss Riley. Then he wanted to disappear behind closed doors and take a nap.

He thought of Brett, and what his brother would expect from him. Then he put a smile on his face and turned toward the voice.

"I think you dropped this." Riley held up a watch, but it certainly wasn't his. Her whole face burst into a smile, and Evan started laughing.

"There you are," he said, grabbing onto her and swinging her around. "Oh, it's so good to see you." He took a deep breath of her skin and hair, getting floral and fruity notes. Everything inside him rejoiced, and he felt himself falling more and more in love with her. He tried to pull himself back from that cliff, but it was useless.

He righted her and swept one arm around her to keep her close. Leaning down, he kissed her right there in the airport. He didn't care who saw. Didn't care if they took pictures on their cell phones and posted them online.

Riley didn't let him get too out of control before she put her hand on his chest and pressed him back. "You made it. How was the flight?"

"Flight was fine," he said, looking around for his bag. He pulled out the handle and secured his free hand in hers. "Tell me you have food nearby."

"At my house." She glanced at him out of the corner

of her eye, and Evan noticed something different about her.

"You're not wearing tons of makeup," he said.

"Yeah," she said. "Going a little more natural these days."

"I like it," he said. "I liked the other eye makeup too. They're both nice."

Riley burst out laughing, and Evan was glad she hadn't taken offense. "I feel like you've changed," she said.

"I haven't. Still me." He stuffed a ballcap on his head as they went outside, and Riley drove them from the airport on the east side of the island to her house which sat on the west coast. He told her why he'd left, and how nothing had really been set in stone as far as a contract went.

She said very little, but she seemed attentive and interested in his business. Why, he wasn't sure. The business side of the band bored him to no end. It was the creating, the writing, the performing that Evan liked.

"Here we are," she said, pulling up to her small house practically swallowed by the jungle.

Evan peered out the windshield. This house was perfectly Riley. He grinned at her and got out of the car, taking in a deep breath of the island air. "It smells so good here," he said.

She led him down a path to the front door, the foliage of Hawaii almost reaching out and touching him. "It's not much," she said. "But I like it." Her house was spotless, of course. Evan wouldn't expect anything less from her. Comfortable couches filled the living room where they stood, and Riley went past them into the kitchen.

"I've been here before," he said, stepping inside and closing the door as the cats started rubbing against him. "Remember I took pictures of the heels?"

"Oh, right."

He followed her into the kitchen, noting that the table was set for four for a reason he couldn't name. In fact, he'd only ever seen that in pictures for vacation rentals or on real estate websites. "The best pizza on the island," she said, bringing his attention back to her. "We can eat on the lanai. You can see the ocean from here."

"Can't wait," he said, picking up a paper plate and loading it with pizza. She led him through a wall of windows to the lanai, which had comfortable patio furniture on it. The view was spectacular, with the ocean seemingly within his reach.

"Wow," he said, drinking in the view. "And it's so quiet."

"I have neighbors," she said. "But they're about fifty feet away."

"Nice." He sat down at the table with her, and they started eating. "How big is it?" he asked.

"Two bedrooms, two bathrooms." She shrugged. "It works for me. It was the first house I bought, and I've fixed it up a little."

"More than a little," he said. "Everything in there is like, brand new."

"It is not." She rolled her eyes. "It's just *clean*, Evan."

"Hey, I have a housekeeper," he said, bursting into laughter in the next moment.

Riley just shook her head and ate her lunch. Evan was supremely glad he'd flown back on a Saturday, because he'd get to see her more. "Tell me what's been going on here," he said.

"Not much," she said. "Same old, same old. There aren't as many tourists on the island right now. That's kind of nice. My friends keep trying to get me to enter the pumpkin-carving contest Sweet Breeze is hosting." She giggled. "But I've seen those pumpkins, and there's no way I'd win."

"Hmm." Evan finished his pizza and wiped his fingers on a paper towel. "Do you only do things you know you'll win?"

Her gaze flew to his, pure shock in those lovely eyes. "Of course not."

"Maybe we should do the carving thing together."

"Can you carve a pumpkin?"

"I mean, I did as a kid."

"Oh, so you're an expert then." She smiled and those eyes glittered, and Evan was so glad to be here with her.

"I missed you, you know." He leaned toward her, beyond thrilled when she met him halfway and kissed him like she missed him too.

Chapter Seventeen

Riley enjoyed kissing Evan. He ignored two phone calls while he explored her mouth, kissed her neck, and whispered sweet things in her ears. Finally, he said, "It's Carl. Can I take this?"

"Do what you need to do," she said, her voice bordering on husky and breathless.

"I didn't tell him I was leaving LA." Evan stood up and swiped on the call. "Hey, brother."

Riley watched him walk back into her tiny house, his height almost too much for her low ceilings. She sighed, because having him back on the island was wonderful. But he hadn't told his brother? Why not?

She could hear him talking in the kitchen, but she didn't try to make out what he was saying. She'd missed him too, and having him back was wonderful. But the fact that he hadn't told his brother he was leaving, and things hadn't been settled with his contracts, meant that he'd be leaving again very soon.

It's fine, she told herself. People had long distance relationships all the time. She had an operational phone, and she and Evan had spoken every day while he'd been in LA. All fifteen of them.

He came back out onto the lanai several minutes later, and she asked, "When are you leaving again?"

He sighed, and she watched the life leave his shoulders. "Monday morning."

"So we have the weekend." She looked at him, trying to feel hopeful. "Want to take that cruise tomorrow?"

"You're not upset?"

"What? Am I going to get upset every time you have to go?" She shrugged. "I don't want to be upset all the time."

"There's just a weird snafu with the label right now," he said.

"I know," Riley said. "I'm not upset." She didn't want to spend their limited time talking about it either. She just wanted to enjoy him while he was here. "Have you been over to Lucky's Lagoon?"

"That sounds risqué," he said, laughing.

"It's the best snorkeling on the island," she said, swatting his bicep. "You're not going to get lucky or anything."

"Shoot," he said, his eyes locking onto hers. The same sparks that had always existed between them heated her blood. "Do I get to see the black swimming suit again?"

"Heavens, no," she said. "I never wear the same swimming suit twice in a row."

"Oh, a mystery suit then."

"Do you have swimming trunks?" she asked. "Snorkel gear?"

"Yes, and no."

"We can rent the gear." She stood up from the patio table. "So come on. You want to spend the afternoon on the beach with me?"

"Absolutely," he said, and Riley let him take her into his arms and hold her against his chest. The moment stilled and lengthened, and Riley remembered how wonderful it was to belong to someone else.

Despite not wanting to get her heart shredded, she really did enjoy belonging to someone. There were so few people on this island she truly felt like she belonged with, and he was one of them.

Clearing her throat, she stepped back. "Okay, let me pack a bag and get changed. Then we'll zip over to your place to get your trunks, and we'll go."

An hour later, Riley and Evan had the perfect spot on the beach. Not too close to the water, so they weren't dealing with splashing children. Not too far away that they couldn't leave their towels to go snorkeling.

Riley had gotten in the water once, just for a few minutes, but really, she wanted to soak up the sun and eat greasy food from the taco stand down the beach a little ways.

When she told her plans to Evan, he didn't respond. "Hey," she said, putting her hand on his forearm. "Are you with me?"

"Huh? Yeah," he said, though his thoughts were clearly somewhere else. He sighed, a long, drawn-out hiss that further testified that he wasn't fine.

"So tacos?" she asked brightly as if she hadn't first lost him to his home in Malibu and then his thoughts.

"Yes," he said, getting up. "Tacos." He pulled her to her feet too and kept his hand secured in hers. "Charlie's always telling me about these tacos."

"Is he?" Riley glanced at Evan. "You haven't said much about him."

"We were roommates in college," Evan said. "He was studying theater, and I did music." Evan smiled, and the action made him twice as handsome as usual. "We got along great, and I kept trying to recruit him for my band. He'd laugh and say there was no band." He chuckled. "I guess I showed him."

Riley giggled too. "I guess you did."

Evan sobered quickly, and his hand in hers tightened. "I wanted—I wondered if I could talk to you about something."

"Of course," Riley said.

"Carl called earlier, and he said TriCities has proposed a solo album."

Riley absorbed the information, trying not to take too long before she responded. "Wow. A solo album. What… do you want to do a solo album?"

"Not particularly," he said. "I'd be nowhere without Georgia Panic, and I've never wanted to strike out on my own." He sighed, and it seemed like even the warm sand beneath his feet couldn't comfort him. "But TriCities doesn't want to offer the band an album. They said—they told Carl—that solo albums are all they're doing right now, but they'll take our songs and *maybe* group them into an album later."

"And you're trying to figure out what to do."

"Yeah." He pulled her closer and put his arm around her waist. Riley sure did like walking side-by-side with him, the tropical paradise where they lived so beautiful and tranquil. People paid thousands of dollars to visit Getaway Bay, and she lived here. Experienced it every day.

"What do you think?" he asked.

"Oh, uh, I think you already know what you want to do."

That sigh again, and Riley liked how conflicted it was. Just because Evan Garfield had a lot of money, a gorgeous voice, and an award that literally made him one of the most sought-after bachelors didn't mean he didn't have problems.

First world problems, sure. But problems, just like the rest of humanity.

"Yeah, I can't do a solo album. I can't do that to my band, for one. And I have no desire to have a solo album, for two."

"Then there's the answer." She smiled up at him. "Now, let's see who can eat the most tacos. I think I'm going to beat you."

Evan tipped his head back and laughed, the sound filling the wide sky above them. Riley liked that she could make him laugh. Liked joking with him and eating far too many tacos just to try to beat him. She didn't, of course, but that afternoon on the beach was absolute perfection.

The time she got with him made it possible for her to say good-bye to him on Monday morning as she dropped him off at the airport. Once again, he didn't have a return date, and Riley wasn't sure when she'd see him again.

So she gripped the collar of his jacket and pulled him down for another kiss. "Good luck in California," she whispered against his neck, glad he seemed to be holding her as tightly as she gripped him.

And then he was gone. Through the sliding glass doors and surely into the line at security. Then on a plane and flying across the ocean, away from her.

She felt like she was mimicking Evan and his long sighs as she turned around and headed back to her car. Riley told herself she hadn't given him her heart, but she felt so hollow inside that she was sure she was lying to herself.

A WEEK PASSED, AND RILEY MADE IT THROUGH THE evening hours without Evan by working late and going home with Charlotte. She and Dawson were such a happy couple, and they were willing to share their take-out and their back porch that overlooked both bays.

She spoke to Evan often, usually at work during lunch or one of her late nights. They texted a lot. But Riley was back to being lonely, and she hated that feeling more than any other.

On the eleventh day of his absence, he called without texting her first. Riley glanced at her phone and then up and over the counter in front of her desk. Their next client would be arriving in fifteen minutes, but maybe he just had some exciting news.

Like maybe that he was coming home.

Home.

Riley couldn't believe she thought of Getaway Bay as his home, and she told herself not to think like that.

She realized she was about to miss his phone call, and she quickly swiped open the call and lifted the phone to her ear. "Hey," she said.

"Riley," he said. "They just asked Georgia Panic to perform at the Super Bowl!" He laughed in the next moment, the sound bright and filled with joy. Even across the distance between them, Riley experienced some of that same happiness in her own soul.

"That's great," she said.

"Thanks," he said. "We're all stoked, and we've told our agent that if TriCities doesn't offer us a contract by the end of the week, he can shop us around. I mean, how many people get to play the *Super Bowl*?"

"Very few, I would imagine," Riley said, trying to make herself sound excited. "Surely they'll offer you an album now."

"They've dug their heels in pretty hard," Evan said. "I don't know what they'll do."

Riley really wanted to ask him when he'd be coming back to Getaway Bay, but she sucked the words back in. Problem was, she didn't know what else to say. Or what to ask him. Everything revolved around what he was doing in California, or her job, and their conversations felt stale. Overused. Unexciting.

"Okay," she said when there was a lull in the conversation. She really had no idea what he'd said, and her mind revolved around what her life would be as autumn continued to march forward.

"So you'll come?" he asked, and Riley's pulse accelerated.

"When, exactly?" she asked.

"Thanksgiving," he said. "At my house in Malibu."

For some reason, tears sprang to her eyes. He wasn't going to come back to Getaway Bay. She shook her head, first at herself for being so stupid as to think he would.

And second, because she didn't want to talk while so much emotion choked her throat.

"Oh, I have to go," he said. "I'll call you back."

"Mm hm," she said, pulling the phone away from her ear and hanging up before he could really hear how upset she was. She sniffled and wiped her eyes, her black makeup coming off slightly.

She hated that makeup. Hated the really dark locks falling down to her waist. Hated that she'd let herself fall for Evan Garfield when she'd known—she'd *known*—he wasn't going to stay in town.

She'd called her stylist weeks ago, but she'd never set an appointment. *Time to do it*, she told herself.

Her phone chimed and she looked numbly down at it. Evan had texted. Before she could swipe open the text, the bell on the front door rang, and Riley sprang to her feet to welcome their next client.

The Chief of Police entered, his daughter right beside him. They'd come to everything at Your Tidal Forever together, because the Chief had lost his wife to cancer a few years ago. Riley always smiled when she saw them, their solidarity so refreshing and comforting. They reminded her that she could get through hard things with the support of her family and friends.

She could weather this storm with Evan too.

"Jennifer," she said, making one more swipe at her eyes to make sure she didn't have any lingering tears. "So good to see you again." She moved around the desk and hugged the bride-to-be. "Chief." She stepped back and shook the man's hand. "Shannon's ready for you in her office. I'll let her know you're coming back."

"Thanks, Riley," the Chief said with a huge smile. Riley picked up the phone and did her job, smiling them down the hall. Then she sat down at her desk and cradled her head in her hands.

Evan had texted, and she checked the message. *I'll be back in a couple of days. Want to celebrate with me?*

She did, and she didn't.

He didn't say he was coming home. And he'd probably stay for a weekend and go back to California. "That's not the life I want," she murmured to herself.

Call me when you can, she typed out, each letter appearing on the screen so slowly. *We need to talk.*

Chapter Eighteen

"We need to talk?" Evan stared at the message from Riley, his heartbeat suddenly racing through his whole system. "That's not good."

"Evan," Hank said, poking his head out of the conference room. "Greg has John on the phone."

Of course he did. They'd been waiting to get their producer from TriCities on the phone for days. Of course he'd call right when Evan had gotten the worst text of his life. "I need a minute," he said.

"Nope," Hank said. "Come on, man. We've been waiting for this for a long time." He was right, and Evan couldn't make his band wait because Riley was going to break up with him. With a heavy heart, he turned and went back into the room.

He barely listened as John and Greg spoke, though everyone else in the room seemed rapt, on the edge of their seats. Evan wasn't sure what had transpired, only that Greg looked up from the speaker phone with a triumphant smile on his face, and DJ high-fived Peter.

So whatever had just been said was good news. Evan smiled too and tried to focus. This was his career. This was important to him. *Riley is too*, his brain whispered, but he shelved the thoughts for now.

Of course Riley was too, but Evan felt like she was unreachable. And he'd done exactly what she'd thought he would. Leave Getaway Bay. Leave her.

He hadn't even given her the six months he'd promised.

His heart felt heavy, and he listened to his agent iron out terms everyone would be happy with. He celebrated with his friends and bandmates, agreed to get together the next day to start working on their set for the Super Bowl, and he went back to the huge Malibu home where no one waited for him.

When he couldn't put off calling Riley any longer, he finally dialed her number. "Hey," he said when she answered. "What's going on?"

"I just…I don't think you should come back this weekend."

"Why not?"

"Because I don't think I can drop you off at the airport and watch you fly out of my life again." She'd always been so direct with him, and Evan appreciated that. "It's not really fair to either of us," she added, her voice a bit pinched now.

"This was not what I intended."

"I know that," she said. "Even the best intentions don't always work out."

Evan nodded, though she wasn't in the room and couldn't see him. "So that's a no for this weekend. What about Thanksgiving?"

"I think—" Her voice cut out, and Evan thought he must've lost the connection. But he checked, and everything was fine. She'd just gone silent.

"Riley, honey?" he asked.

"Don't," she said.

"I'm sorry," he said, unsure of what else he could possibly say.

"I think it's a no for everything, Evan." She spoke with authority now. "You probably have a ton of things to do to get ready to play for the Super Bowl."

The band did want to start on a new song right away, debut it at the big game. Evan didn't know what to do now. It was rare for him to not have something to say, some way to fill the silence. He could charm sixty thousand people with just a guitar and a microphone.

Why didn't he know what to say to this woman?

"Okay, I have to go," Riley said. "I have a client in a few minutes."

"Yeah, okay," he said. "Bye." The call ended, and Evan felt like a complete fool. He stared at his device like the phone would ring again, and Riley would tell him what had just happened was all a joke.

"What's a joke, Evan," he told himself as he stood up. "Is that you've been in Getaway Bay for two days out of the past twenty-six. No wonder she broke up with you." He shoved his phone in his back pocket and went into the music studio he kept here at the Malibu home. He'd brought all of his notes and sheet music from Hawaii, and he stared at the song he'd been writing for Riley.

Part of him wanted to crumple all the pages and throw them in the trash. To save himself from himself, he left the music room and went out to the garage. He had a couple of motorcycles here, and he just wanted to ride.

Carl wouldn't like it, but Evan didn't like much about his life at the moment. So he grabbed a helmet and the keys to a sleek, navy blue motorcycle, and he left the house in the Malibu hills behind. If only it was as easy to leave other things behind.

OF COURSE, EVAN COULDN'T OUTRUN ANYTHING, EVEN on a motorcycle. He'd learned that during his divorce from Kitty. He went to the meetings Carl told him to, and he met Brett's girlfriend. He'd called his parents and asked them to come to Malibu, and they'd agreed. So he hosted Thanksgiving dinner at his house in California, and the whole band and their significant others came.

He was really tired of being a couple with Carl, but he hadn't dared to reach out to Riley again. She'd been quite clear in how she felt about their relationship.

He laid awake most nights for at least an hour before

he could get himself to turn his brain off enough to fall asleep. He'd tap out texts to Riley to tell her something that had happened before he realized they weren't speaking.

Sometimes, while he sipped his coffee, he'd scroll through their old text stream and read the conversations they used to have. The hole inside him seemed to widen inch by inch until he felt like someone had hollowed him out with a spade.

"Hey," Carl asked one day when Evan finally stumbled down to the kitchen for coffee. He wasn't sure what day of the week it was, or what time it was. "We still have that place in Hawaii. What are you doing with that?"

"I'm going for the wedding," Evan said, stirring some sugar into his coffee. Didn't Carl know he couldn't talk to Evan until after he'd had his coffee? "So we'll stay there then, and then I'll let it go."

"Really?" The incredulity in Carl's voice got Evan to abandon the sugar bowl.

"Yeah, really."

"Odd."

"Odd, how?" Evan watched his brother, because Carl was very bad at hiding how he felt about things.

"What about you and Riley?" he asked. "Seemed like you two were getting serious."

"I don't want to talk about Riley," Evan said, probably for the tenth time. "She's—"

"Off-limits," he and Carl said together, his brother

adding, "I know. But, come on, Evan. You're a complete mess since things ended with her."

"I am not," Evan said. "I go to every meeting you set up for me. I'm working on the new song. Heck, we'll be ready to record it before Christmas."

Carl shook his head, displeasure on his face. The same look Evan had seen on his face when he'd grabbed his keys to go pick Riley up at work or take her lunch. The furrowed eyebrows, the semi-angry glint in his eye.

"I don't understand why you're upset with me," Evan said.

"I'm not," Carl said. "I've just seen Brett with Skye, and you with Riley, and you guys seemed…happy. I was thinking…." He trailed off and cleared his throat.

Evan stared at Carl. "You've been thinking you want a girlfriend." He couldn't believe he was speaking these words, but there they were.

"I mean, maybe," Carl said, so falsely that Evan started laughing. It almost sounded happy, and Evan almost felt like himself again.

Almost.

"Maybe we should keep the house," Carl said. "I'm thinking of taking a step away from the band, and I might want to see if I can find someone on the island the way you did. Hey, maybe I'll lose my watch on the flight there."

"Taking a step away from the band?" Evan asked, trying to process everything his brother had just said.

Keep the house.

Step away from the band.

Find someone on the island.

Lose my watch.

Evan's mind started buzzing, but Carl said, "Yeah, I love working with you and Brett, but the Panic could hire a new manager. I don't do anything special."

"You keep me sane," Evan said, lifting his mug to his lips. "And on time to everything. And…." How could he say he couldn't imagine being managed by someone besides his brother?

"And maybe you could hire a certain dark-haired woman to keep you sane and on time to everything," Carl said. "I mean, isn't that what Riley does?"

"No," Evan said, but that buzzing started again. His thoughts whirred, and he couldn't make sense of them. The underlying message wailed though, sort of a low scream that took him several seconds to understand.

Get Riley back.

"I need to get her back," he said out loud.

"That's the spirit," Carl said. "So we'll keep the house?"

"How am I going to do that?" Evan asked.

"Well," Carl said nonchalantly, as if he hadn't thought about it at all. "You can start with that song you've been working on in secret."

"That's private," Evan said, instant anger springing through him.

"I know," Carl said. "I haven't looked at it. I just heard you playing it the other day." He cut a glance at

Evan out of the corner of his eye. "It was a beautiful song, and that's when I knew you were in love with her."

Evan scoffed. "I'm not…in love…." He met his brother's eye, his emotions suddenly too overwhelming for him. "Do you think she'll talk to me?"

"No, bro," Carl said. "I think you need a solid plan to let her know how you feel. Chocolate. The woman likes chocolate, right? And a million different ways to say you're sorry."

"I already said I was sorry."

"And a job offer," Carl said as if Evan hadn't spoken. "And that song ready, and a plan to make sure she can travel with you and the band, be by your side, whatever she needs. Because I know she doesn't like being left behind."

"How do you know that? Have you been talking to her?"

"No," Carl said. "I know, because I'm just like her." He gave Evan a pointed look and said, "We have a meeting with that reporter from Vibe in an hour. You better get caffeinated and showered."

"I don't want to meet with them," Evan said.

"Deal with it, bud," Carl said. "You only become a billionaire once."

Evan rolled his eyes. "I'm not joining that billionaire club or whatever that was on the island."

"Yes, you are," Carl said as he walked out of the kitchen. "One hour."

Evan wanted to protest, but he always ended up

doing what his brother set up for him. So he'd meet with the reporter from Vibe, and he'd join the Nine-0 Club in Getaway Bay—and hopefully, he'd get Riley back too.

Now he just needed to do all of the things Carl had listed to get her back, and that meant he could caffeinate, shower, *and* practice the song he'd written for Riley.

Chapter Nineteen

Riley kept her head down as she got off the plane. She'd see her family soon enough, and then she'd be plunged into that chaos. She hadn't gone to Oahu for Thanksgiving, but Hope had insisted she take a few days off before Christmas and the big Pyne wedding.

"Riley!"

She looked up at the high, child's voice that called her name. Her niece, Winnie, held up a big sign with her initials on it, and Riley burst into a grin. She started walking faster, scooping the seven-year-old into her arms with a laugh.

"Hey, Winnie-bear," she said, holding onto the little girl. "Thanks for coming to get me at the airport."

"Mama went to get a drink," she said. "Daddy's right there."

"Aloha, Sissy." Her older brother Jason slung his arm around her. "How was the flight?"

"Oh, you know. It's an hour." Riley didn't want to think about the last flight she'd been on from Oahu back to Getaway Bay. She grinned up at her brother. "How is everyone?"

"It's much quieter on the island without everyone here," Jason said. "You're smart to come when no one else is here."

Riley didn't say that was why she hadn't come for Thanksgiving. She'd promised her mother she'd come before the wedding and the Christmas holiday, and here she was. Of course, then she'd have to face her mother alone, but Riley hadn't usually had a problem with her mom.

"Mama's got her sticky rice on," Jason said. "Winnie is so excited to show you her new lizard, and you have to act surprised, but Kelly is pregnant again."

"What?" Riley stopped, hope entering her heart. "Are you kidding me right now?" Tears came to her eyes, because Kelly and Jason had been trying to have another baby for five years. Riley understood waiting for something she wanted desperately, and she grabbed onto her brother and wept into his shoulder. "Congratulations."

"You told her, didn't you?"

Riley let go of Jason and grabbed only Kelly. "I'm so happy for you."

"I'm sorry," Jason said. "I'm just so excited."

"When are you due?" Riley asked, stepping back and looking at Kelly.

"Not until July," Kelly said. "We've only told my parents and yours." She glared at Jason. "We don't want to have to tell everyone if we lose another baby."

"Riley gets it," Jason said. "That's why she didn't tell anyone about her rockstar boyfriend."

Pure horror struck her behind her lungs. "Where did you hear that?"

"I think you forget that I used to live in Getaway Bay," Jason said, both of his eyebrows raised.

"I broke up with the rockstar a long time ago," Riley said, feeling every day of Evan's absence. "I can't even remember his name."

"That is so not true," Kelly said, reaching for Winnie's hand. "Your aunt is a big, fat liar." She grinned at Riley, who suddenly felt like crying again. She hated that weakness in her, and that the feelings of sadness over losing Evan had lingered for so long. Lisa had tried to tell her she'd fallen for Evan, and maybe she had. Riley didn't want to acknowledge it, because then she'd never get over him.

She'd watched the Super Bowl halftime announcement, and she'd followed the news of a new contract for Georgia Panic, which had come in the form of the largest contract for a band in the past three years.

She'd smiled while she'd cried as she read the Internet article. As she thought about Evan in Malibu. As she remembered his bond with his brothers and bandmates.

Then she'd pull herself together and go to work. Keep everything together for as long as she could, and then escape to the beach. When she finally went home, she was glad she didn't have to use a dozen makeup remover wipes to get her eyeliner off.

"I love your natural look, though," Kelly said, and Riley smiled at her gratefully.

"Thanks, Kel. I feel more like myself again." She'd given up the extensions and the hair dye. She'd gone through a few weeks there where she'd pulled her hair up and worn a cute hat to work to get through the transition from dark back to red.

She liked her hair now, and she was so grateful for a stylist who was as patient as she was talented. When she looked in the mirror now, she could see her freckles. Her green eyes matched her red hair better than the black. And she was starting to find herself again.

Maybe.

Slowly.

She rode in the backseat with Winnie to her parents' house, where her mother and father waited on the lanai. "Mama," she said as she got out of the car. She went to the patio and hugged her mom. "How are you?"

She loved how tight her mother hugged, and then she embraced her father too, glad she'd come. Even though she'd basically been forced to take time off and Lisa had almost booked her airplane ticket for her.

"When's the wedding?" her mom asked, and Riley's heart jumped over itself. For one terrible moment, she thought maybe her mother was asking when Riley's wedding was.

Never.

"Uh, next Friday," Riley said. "I'm going back Thursday morning to be ready." She ignored the flicker of panic inside her of all that needed to be done before the wedding. Lisa and Shannon had assured her everything would be set, and that she needed to take a few days away.

"Not just from the office," Lisa had said. "But from Getaway Bay."

What she really meant was Riley needed to stop obsessing over Evan and whether he'd be back on the island for the wedding. Of course he would be. Charlie and Amelia had both confirmed that Evan would still be singing at the wedding. All that meant for Riley was that she needed to stay behind the scenes so she wouldn't see him.

She didn't think she'd run into him. After all, he was the talent and would surely be kept in isolation until it was time to sing. Then he'd get ushered onto the scene and bustled away. She may or may not have watched some Internet videos of some of his performances, but she was taking that knowledge to the grave.

"Dinner is ready," her mother said. "Come eat, come eat." Her mother's favorite thing to do was feed people, and Riley wasn't going to deprive her of that over the next five days.

"I love you," Riley said to her mom on Thursday morning. "Thanks for taking such good care of me." She smiled down on her aging mother, noting how gray she'd gotten. But she'd had an amazing week with her mom and dad. They'd laughed. They'd cried. She'd told them about Evan, and they'd talked about her job as they watched dogs trot past the house.

Riley returned to Getaway Bay, determined not to look at the ground until she returned to Your Tidal Forever. That way, she couldn't see any watches that sexy rockstars had dropped, and then replaced, before she contacted them.

She'd worn her work clothes on the plane, and she went straight to the office to find out where things stood.

She walked in, and no one rose from the desk where she usually sat. The air conditioning hummed along, and the water fountain buzzed, and the phone rang. Her heartbeat skipped, but before she could even take one step to answer it, the peal silenced.

Someone else had answered it.

She wasn't needed here.

Despair filled her, and she hurried to her desk, almost collapsing into her chair. Her tears were just there, appearing out of nowhere and flowing down her face before she could even think about what state her makeup would be in.

"Oh."

Riley looked up when someone spoke, and she found Lisa standing there, a stack of folders in her hand.

"You're back. I didn't hear the door." She dropped the folders and drew Riley into a hug. "What's wrong? Something with your mom and dad?" She held Riley tight and rubbed her back, and Riley really wanted to be needed.

She *needed* to be needed.

Riley shook her head and couldn't speak. Lisa didn't try to suggest anything else. She just held Riley until she quieted, at which point she stepped back and turned away from her best friend.

"I'm sorry," she said. "I'm just…I feel so stupid. I'm fine." She tugged on the bottom of her blouse and sat down. "These are new clients?"

"Just a bunch of invoices we got paid on," Lisa said. "Let's go to lunch later, okay?"

"Okay," Riley said, but she knew Lisa had appointments during lunch. After all, just because Riley had gone off-island didn't mean she didn't have access to her calendar.

She drew in a deep breath and focused. Filing first. She loved filing, and maybe she'd be able to figure out why she'd broken down because someone else had answered the phone.

———

The next day, Riley did her best to stay out of the way. She arranged flowers early and disappeared inside the staging tent the closer to the wedding start time. She wore a pretty floral dress like everyone else at Your Tidal Forever, and she kept her smile cemented in place so no one would know she was dying a slow death inside.

Evan was supposed to sing before the actual ceremony, and then again during the dancing portion. As the crowd rose and the bride glided down the aisle to her waiting groom, Riley caught sight of the handsome man that had turned her life upside down.

"Good afternoon, everyone," he said, his voice like pure butter. Smooth and Southern and absolutely sexy. Her heart pounded in her chest, and she couldn't look away from him in that form-fitted tuxedo, his hair all swept up in a casual-not-casual beach look.

"We're here to celebrate Charlie and Amelia, and I'm going to sing a song I wrote just for them."

Riley swooned—along with every other female in the vicinity, married or not. In that moment, she realized three things.

One, she wanted Evan Garfield in her life again.

Two, she needed to apologize to him for being so demanding.

Three, she was in love with him. One-hundred-percent in love with him.

She pressed one hand to her racing pulse as he continued to speak. "But that song is going to come after this one." He cleared his throat. "This song I actually wrote for my girlfriend. Well, she was my girlfriend, and I kinda messed things up with her." He smiled around at the crowd. "Have you ever done that?"

A collective "Yeah," went up from the wedding party, but Riley couldn't look away from Evan. Was he talking about her? Or had he found someone else in California and messed things up with them?

"Well, you should know I'm just a guy, and I made some mistakes too. I miss her like crazy, though, and I've somehow convinced myself that if I sing her this song here at this wedding, she'll forgive me and take me back." He scanned the crowd again, but Riley knew she stood out of his sight.

Lisa elbowed her and hissed, "Go out there," but Riley shook her head no. She wasn't into public displays of affection, especially at someone else's wedding.

"Okay, I'm ready," Evan said, and someone handed him a guitar. He set the microphone in the stand and adjusted the shoulder strap on his guitar. He was gorgeous and full of light in the moment before he opened his mouth, and then the most glorious sound came out.

The song was a ballad, perfect for slow-dancing, and all of her doubts about who this song was for flew away when she heard the first line.

She sits in the coffee shop, her head bent down

Tears gathered in Riley's eyes, and her pulse thundered in her veins, and she felt frozen to the beach beneath her feet.

She's lovely in the sun, and perfect in the rain, and if I ever see her again

I'll tell her that I love her.

If I ever see her again

I'll tell her that I love her.

The last notes and chords combined together, and Riley realized she wasn't the only one with wet eyes.

"Get out there right now," Lisa said. "And tell him you love him too."

The crowd clapped, and Evan handed off his guitar and bowed for them. Riley wasn't sure if she was pushed or if she started walking, but she exited the safety of the tent where she and the other women had stored their bins for setup.

"I don't know if that worked," Evan said. "But I'd just like to say I'm sorry to—" He cut off when Charlie Pyne stepped next to him and pointed at Riley.

Evan turned and looked, and Riley's eyes met his. Time seemed to slow into nothing, and everyone and everything fell away.

"Riley," he said, now suddenly in front of her. "I love you."

She looked up at him, every cell inside her bursting with energy, with the love he'd given her. "I love you, too."

"Yeah?" He grinned and cradled her face in both of his hands. "I'm so sorry."

"Kiss her!" someone in the crowd yelled, and Riley giggled through her tears. And kissing Evan when she knew he loved her was even more magical than she'd ever imagined.

She kissed him while people she didn't know whooped and cheered. She kissed him while she cried. She kissed him like she was in love with him—because she was.

Chapter Twenty

Evan hadn't been sure until the moment Charlie had stepped up to him and pointed that Riley would respond to his song. His heart still thrashed around inside his chest like he'd tried to remove it from his body against its will.

Singing so openly like that. With so much emotion. So much vulnerability.

Evan didn't normally do that, at least not in public.

He pulled away from Riley and ran his hands through her hair. "I like this new color," he whispered.

"We should get off the stage," she whispered back. "So Amelia and Charlie can get married."

Alarm moved through him. "Right." He stepped over to Charlie and hugged him hard. "Thank you for letting me have a minute."

"Love you, brother." Charlie pounded him on the back, and Evan took Riley's hand and they got off the stage. She tugged him inside a tent filled with other women, all of them sniffling.

"My friends at work," she said, but Evan had met all of them before. "You remember them?"

"Of course," he said, putting on his rockstar smile even though his hopes were falling, crashing, burning.

Riley would never leave Getaway Bay. Her perfect job that she was really good at. Her friends.

So he'd sung a pretty song and gotten her back, but it felt temporary. Carl's voice in the back of his mind told him to *be honest. Get everything out in the open with Riley as soon as possible.*

For once, Evan was glad his brother liked to discuss everything to death before letting it go.

"Riley," he said, facing her again. She was beautiful with that red hair, the fresh face. "I am in love with you, but I don't see how our relationship can work with us as we are now."

She sucked in a breath, her smile vanishing as easily as if he'd flipped a switch.

"Don't say anything yet," he said. "I know you need time to process things. I know you're working. I'm back on the island through the New Year, and Carl and I are keeping the house here. But you have to know I won't be here all that much."

His throat hurt, and he needed a drink, but he had to say this first. "Carl's quitting as band manager for Georgia Panic. We need someone who's as detailed as he is. As meticulous in their professionalism. Who won't take crap from anyone."

"I'll take the job," Lisa said, stepping slightly in front of Riley.

Evan grinned at her, glad she'd said that, though he hadn't even asked her to.

"No, I want it," Charlotte said.

"Hey," Shannon said. "I think I'm the most qualified."

Evan wanted to hug all of these women. He couldn't have planned this job offer more perfectly. He looked around at all of them, and it seemed like they'd crawled right inside his head, because they all looked at Riley simultaneously.

"I want you," he said, clearing his throat. "I want to offer the job to you, Riley."

Tears filled her eyes, and she shook her head. Pure panic paraded through him, but he remained still and silent. Riley always needed more time than him to make decisions, especially big ones. And this one was huge.

Her smile indicated she wasn't telling him no. She just didn't believe what was happening.

"It pays pretty well," he said. "And you'd travel with the band. Be wherever the band is. Of course, you'd have to maintain a home somewhere…and I hear you have a great place with an amazing view of the nightly sunsets on the island." He grinned at her. "Like I said, I know you need time to think about things. I know it would be a huge change for you. I know you're working right now."

He released her hand and fell back a step. "Heck, I have to go work right now." He touched his palm over his heart and added, "After the wedding, I'll be at my house. Come by anytime—if you want."

And with that, he left the tent so he could watch one of his good friends get married. Doubts streamed through him, but he pretended like everything was right and had worked out. Of course it wasn't. He knew better than most that pretty words were just that—words. Songs were just songs. Music was powerful for him, but Riley needed actions to tell her how he felt.

He'd tried to give her that. He was keeping the house—renting it for now—and he'd offered her the job. He'd said everything he needed to say.

Now she got to decide.

Charlie and Amelia's wedding was beautiful, and it made Evan's heart happy to see his friend so in love. The sight of their wedded bliss also reminded him of how much he loved Riley. He hadn't seen her again during the wedding, but that was simply a sign of the professionalism of the staff at Your Tidal Forever.

He'd sung for the first dance, and he'd stayed through the cake cutting. He'd ridden his motorcycle home, his tuxedo jacket flapping in the wind.

Carl had been on the pool deck, wearing his swimming trunks and tapping on his phone. Evan took one look at him and said, "I'm changing. Be right back."

"How did it go?" Carl called after him, but Evan just waved his hand. After he'd changed and sprayed himself with sunscreen, he sat beside Carl.

His brother said nothing, which was an open door for Evan to start the conversation. He took a deep breath, and said, "I sang the song."

"And?"

"And she came out and we made up." Evan smiled just thinking about that kiss. "I offered her the job. She'll take her time to think about it."

Carl let a couple of beats of silence go by. "She better hurry up, because I already have two dates." He twisted his phone toward Evan. "This Getaway Bay Singles app is pretty slick."

"Oh, you set it up already?"

"Yeah," Carl said. "And I've already been messaging several people." His phone chimed, and he turned it back toward him. "I'm meeting someone at the coffee shop where you met Riley. So you know, maybe it'll be a good place." He smiled at Evan, and Evan couldn't remember the last time Carl looked so relaxed.

"Thanks for all you've done for the band," Evan said, his emotions touching his voice again. "For me."

"Of course," Carl said, looking away from the phone. Their eyes met, and a quiet, brotherly understanding moved between them.

Evan sighed and leaned his head back. "I hope she shows up soon."

"You invited her back here?"

"I told her I knew she had a lot to think about, and that yeah, I'd be by the pool later."

Carl didn't say anything, and Evan glanced over to find him completely engrossed in the dating app. Another smile touched his mouth, and Evan silently prayed that Carl could find someone as amazing as Riley to fall in love with.

The afternoon wore on, and Riley still didn't show up. Worry began to gnaw at Evan. Maybe he'd asked too much of her, too quickly. She would be leaving the island where she'd lived for a very long time. Her friends. Her job. Her family on nearby Oahu. Her two cats.

No, the cats could come.

He practically dove for his phone, realizing he'd left it on silent during the wedding. But Riley hadn't texted or called.

You can bring Sunshine and Marbles on tour, he tapped out quickly. Before he could second-guess himself, he sent the text and relaxed again. Or tried to. The wedding had ended an hour ago. Maybe longer.

Where was she?

Evan must have dozed off, because the next thing he knew, someone was saying his name, and a cool hand touched his face.

He startled and yelped, sitting up and swatting the touch away at the same time.

"Hey, it's okay," a woman said. "It's just me."

"Riley?" He blinked the exhaustion out of his eyes and focused on the beautiful redhead in front of him. It was her, and she was wearing the softest smile he'd ever seen.

"I didn't mean to scare you," she said. "Carl said I could come out here."

"Of course you can." He looked over her shoulder for his brother, and Riley followed his gaze.

"He said he was meeting someone for coffee."

"What time is it?" Evan asked, wiping his hand down his face. His skin felt too hot, and his stomach grumbled for food.

"Almost six," she said. "I had a ton of work to do after the wedding. Sorry I didn't text."

"It's okay." She was here, and Evan could barely believe that. "So…where are we?"

"You know I can't quit my job tomorrow, right? Hope needs to find someone else; I need to train them…." She let her words trail off, and that blasted hope started writhing in Evan's bloodstream again.

"But you're thinking about accepting my job offer," he said.

"Have you talked to the band about it?" she asked.

"Absolutely," he said. "And Carl is willing to stay on until you're ready. He can train you right up too."

"They don't even know me."

"*I* know you," he said. "I've seen you work at Your Tidal Forever. You're perfect for this job."

"What if you, I don't know, get sick of me?"

"Riley." He took both of her hands in his. "That's not going to happen. Maybe you didn't hear the song? I'd ask you to marry me right now if I didn't think you'd freak out and never speak to me again."

Her eyes widened, and Evan chuckled. "See? If anything, I think it's you who will get sick of me. I'm not easy to manage." He knew that he relied on Carl for a lot. A pang of sadness hit him that his brother wouldn't be with the band anymore, but he also knew Carl needed a shot at a more normal life.

"Yeah, I've heard that, actually," Riley said dryly. She squeezed his hands. "I want the job, but I have a lot to do before I'm ready to leave the island. I need to figure out how to take care of my house while I'm not living in it. I need to tie up all the loose ends at work. I need to rehome the cats. I need to talk to my family." She looked worried, and that was the last thing Evan wanted to do to her.

"You can bring the cats," he said. "Hank travels with his dog."

"I don't want to bring the cats," she said. "I think they'll be too much trouble."

"But you love the cats," Evan said, drawing her into his chest. Her body was warm, and he inhaled the fruity scent of her hair. "I don't want to make your life harder. I just want us to be together, and this was the way I thought it would all work out. I'm open to other suggestions."

"Does Carl really want to quit?" she whispered. "I don't want to take his job from him just because you want us to be together."

"He wants to quit," Evan said. "He's on a date right now, because he saw how happy I was when I was with you."

Riley snuggled deeper into his side. "I want the job, Evan. I just have a few things to take care of first."

"I'll take care of the cats on the road," he said.

She giggled, and Evan sure liked the sound of that. "No," she said. "I'm okay rehoming the cats. I love them, but I love you more." She tipped her head back so Evan could kiss her, and as he touched his lips to hers, pure happiness filled him.

Riley kissed him back, the same passion that had always been in her touch present now. So their time apart hadn't set them too far back, and Evan was glad about that too.

"Okay," she said, pulling away. "I'm so hot. Do you want to swim?"

"Sure," he said as she got up. He watched her peel her coverup over her head, revealing a bright yellow bikini that rendered him mute.

She struck a pose and said, "What do you think of this swimming suit?"

Chapter Twenty-One

A couple of weeks later, Riley stapled the bill to the invoice showing it had been paid. "Then these two go together, and you put them in the client's file." She handed the paperwork to Sunny, the new receptionist Hope had hired. She'd been shadowing Riley for two days, and she was as bright as her name suggested. Hungry. Happy.

She reminded Riley so much of herself, and while she nearly started crying every time she thought about leaving Your Tidal Forever, she knew she'd made the right decision. Change was just hard sometimes. All the time, maybe. Riley wasn't sure.

Evan had assured her that she would still need her pencil skirts and heels, her jewelry and makeup, and that she'd get to meet and talk to plenty of people as she arranged everything for Georgia Panic.

He'd been giving her a new band T-shirt every day

since Christmas, because he said they always traveled in "band attire." She'd been slightly surprised to learn that meant Panic T-shirts and jeans, but she was willing to roll with it.

Carl had started to show her a few things in the evenings, and she only had three more days before she officially became the band manager. Carl had agreed to stay on through the Super Bowl to make sure she was comfortable and nothing got dropped during the next five weeks.

Riley was extremely grateful, and she told him so every time she saw him or messaged him. Sure, he might have a fierce look about him, and bark a little loud sometimes, but she'd learned that someone had to when it came to keeping five talented musicians on schedule, popular with the public, and feeling good about themselves.

Riley worked with eleven consultants at Your Tidal Forever, as well as Hope and Shannon, so she was actually downsizing by only having to worry about five people.

She continued to show Sunny how she'd organized the files, and the woman took notes on her phone. "Of course, you can do what you want," Riley said. "This is just how I've done it."

"It's great," Sunny said with a smile. "I don't see why I'd change it."

An alarm on Riley's phone sounded, and she glanced at the note. "Oh, it's my cats. I have to run home and meet the person who's taking them. Are you okay here?"

Alarm ran across Sunny's face. "Alone?"

Riley grinned at her. "Yes, alone. You realize we only have three more days together? Then you'll be running this place." She took Sunny by the shoulders. "And yes, Hope owns the company. Shannon is second-in-command. But Sunny, *you* run this place. Don't forget that." Riley had forgotten it once, and her life had spiraled out of control.

Sunny nodded, and Riley bent to grab her purse from the bottom desk drawer. "You just answer the phone if it rings. We don't have any clients coming in this week. Okay?"

"Okay."

"Great." Riley clicked her way out the front door and hurried back to her house. She had Sunshine's and Marbles's food all packed up. Their cat gym. Their mouse toys. Their beds. She arrived before Vera, the woman who she'd found to take the cats permanently, and Riley was glad she had one more opportunity to say good-bye to them.

Marbles waited by the front door, meowing as Riley entered her house. "Hey." She scooped the gray cat into her arms and glanced around for Sunshine. The orange cat appeared in the mouth of the hallway leading down to the bedrooms, and Riley almost started crying again. "Were you laying on the bed?"

Of course the cat was. It was Sunshine's favorite spot,

because Riley had a window that let in the afternoon sunlight. Sunshine liked to bask in it for her fourth or fifth afternoon catnap.

Riley picked up Sunshine too and buried her face in cat fur. "I'm going to miss you guys," she said. "But Vera is awesome, and I've met her. She loves cats, and she has two other cats already."

She had a flash of herself as a cat lady, and she set the felines down as tires crunched over the gravel out in front of her house. "She's here. You guys be nice to her." She grabbed Sunshine before the female cat could bolt, and she put her in a cat carrier on the couch. "Marbles, you can stay out if you don't run off."

The gray and white cat sat down as if he understood what Riley had said to him. She stepped over to the door and opened it to find Vera getting out of her car. "Hello," she called, and Vera repeated the greeting as she came up the steps.

"They're ready for you," Riley said. "I have food, beds, toys." She picked up the box with the food and started toward Vera's car. "Sunshine is already in the carrier."

"I'll get the gym." Vera picked up the cat climbing toy and followed Riley. Within minutes, everything was in the car, and Vera had Marbles in her arms. "Are you sure you don't want me to pay you?"

"Nope," Riley said. "Just love them." She reached out and stroked Marbles's head. "You be good. No yowling." Marbles meowed, and it sounded so mournful. Riley backed up a step, because she didn't want to show Vera how sad she was to get rid of her cats.

"They'll be well-loved," Vera said, and she ducked into her car. Riley turned and went back up her steps to the safety of her porch. As Vera pulled out, the roar of a motorcycle filled the air, and Riley looked for Evan.

She didn't want to be teary or crying when he arrived, so she wiped her face and hurried inside, closing the door behind her. She barricaded herself in the bathroom and looked into her own eyes. "This is a good thing," she reminded herself. And it was. She knew it was.

"Sweetheart?" Evan called, and she liked that he just entered her house when he arrived.

"Coming," she said back. Then she squared her shoulders and went to greet him.

"Hey, what's wrong?" He took her into his arms, and Riley wasn't sure what he'd seen that she hadn't been able to hide. "Did the cats get off okay?"

"Yes, they just left." She let him hold her, the strength of his arms and body just what she needed.

"I'm sorry," he murmured. "I told you we could keep them."

"I know." She peered up into his face. "I'm fine. I am." She smiled and touched her mouth to his. "Now, take me to dinner, because Carl texted a while ago and said he had a *ton* of work to go through with me tonight."

Several days later, she entered Your Tidal Forever, and Sunny looked up from the front desk. "Riley." She came around and hugged Riley. "What are you doing here? I thought you were leaving today."

"I am. I'm just here to give Lisa my keys." She glanced down the hallway. "Is she in? She said she'd be here."

"Yep, she is." Sunny hurried back to her desk. "I'll tell her you're coming back." Her blue eyes sparkled as she dialed the phone and chirped, "Lisa, Riley's on her way to you."

Riley grinned and went down the hallway, feeling sort of strange she didn't have the accompaniment of heel-clicking as she walked. But it was travel day for Georgia Panic, and that meant she wore blue jeans and a Panic T-shirt. She also wore sneakers, as they were traveling to Nashville today, and the high was supposed to be forty-six-degrees when they landed.

Forty-six. Riley didn't even know what that cold of a temperature felt like, and she shivered as she entered Lisa's office. The blonde was already walking toward the door, and she engulfed Riley in a hug.

"I'm going to miss you so much," she said.

"I'll miss you too," Riley said, holding on to her best friend. She cleared her throat several seconds later and stepped back. "Okay, this is for the mail." She held up her small ring of keys. "I've asked them to hold it and only deliver on Mondays." She switched keys. "This one is for the front door. This one's for the back." She handed the keys to Lisa, who took them and wiped her eyes.

"Who am I going to talk to about my lame dates?"

Riley shook her head and smiled. "Me, silly. I have a phone. And you'll meet someone, I just know it."

"That last guy was a loser."

"I know, honey." Riley hugged her again. Lisa had been so excited about him too, and Riley had never even learned the guy's name before Lisa had broken up with him. "But if someone can fall in love with me, you'll have no trouble finding someone." She grinned at her through the tears and hugged her again.

They'd already had a good-bye party for Riley on Friday, and she suddenly wanted to get out of the building before she saw anyone else. "Okay, Evan's waiting, so I guess I have to go." She backed up toward the door. "The car is in the garage. The keys for it are in the drawer next to the fridge. Take it out every once in a while, okay?"

"You got it," Lisa said with a smile.

And just like that, Riley walked out of Your Tidal Forever, a place she'd called home for eight years. She felt great as she entered the sunshine. And when she found Evan leaning against the passenger side of the car where she'd left him, everything was right in the world.

"Ready?" he asked when he saw her.

"Ready."

Super Bowl night:

Riley watched from the wings, a place she was very good at being. Over the last few weeks, she'd been right at Carl's side as he showed her the ropes. He had a very busy job, but he claimed it ebbed and flowed. She knew exactly what that was like, as Your Tidal Forever had busy seasons and calmer ones.

And right now, Georgia Panic was all the rage. The stage was set. The lights were off. The crowd was going wild.

All they were waiting for was the spotlight to appear on Evan, and then his cool, clear voice would fill the night. The anticipation built and built, and even Riley's pulse felt erratic.

The light burst to life.

Evan's voice rang out, and if possible, the screaming intensified.

Riley grinned at her boyfriend, because he was incredible. Simply incredible. He deserved solo albums and group albums and everything in the world.

He finished the first song, and she waited for Dan to start the next guitar rift. He didn't. Riley straightened, because something was wrong.

Evan stepped back up to the mic, and he said, "Hello, everybody!" The crowd responded with a "Hel-lo," just like they always did at a Georgia Panic concert. Riley hadn't known that until Carl had told her and she'd watched a few fan videos online.

But usually, Dan played a melody behind it. He didn't

tonight, and Riley turned to Carl. "Something's going on with Dan's guitar."

"I'll check on it," he said, and he walked away.

Evan stood at the mic, and he said, "We're going to get things kicked off here real soon. I have one thing I want to do tonight, and I want all of you, and the millions watching around the world, to participate in it with me. Are you ready?"

The crowd loved Evan, and Riley could feel his charisma and charm from her spot dozens of feet away. No wonder they had millions of followers on social media and every song they released went to number one.

"We've got a couple of new songs for you tonight, most that you can buy and download. But there's one special song that you won't be able to get anywhere but here, tonight. I'm going to get a special guest out on the stage with me in a minute, and everyone will know why."

Dan started playing then, and relief hit Riley. She hadn't heard Evan talk about a special guest though, and she was as rapt to the happenings on stage as everyone else in the stadium.

The tune changed, and Riley's pulse flipped right before Evan sang, "She sits in the coffee shop, her head bent down."

"No," she whispered, and Carl appeared in front of her.

"Ma'am, I need you to come with me."

"Carl, I am not going out there," she said, digging her heels in though he hadn't touched her. Every muscle felt tense, and Riley couldn't believe Evan was doing this. She didn't want to be on national TV.

She's lovely in the sun, and perfect in the rain, and if I ever see her again

I'll ask her to marry me.

If I ever see her again

I'll ask her to marry me.

"What?" she asked, looking at the stage as the lyrics repeated themselves. *Marry me.*

"Riley," Carl said. "If you don't come with me now, we anger everyone." He took her by the hand, and she was so stunned she went.

"Ah, here she is," Evan said, the relief evident in his voice. He wasted no time dropping to his knees and positively bellowing into the microphone, "Riley Randall, the love of my life. Will you marry me?"

As if the crowd had been coached, they started chanting, "Say yes, say yes, say yes!"

Say—yes.

Riley's heart beat with the rhythm of the chanting, and Evan held the mic out to her. She was going to kill him when they found themselves alone. Positively kill him.

At the same time, the warm sense of love flowed through her and over her, and she leaned forward and said, "Yes."

The crowd cheered, and Evan swooped her into a kiss which he broke very quickly. "All right! Time to get this show started!"

The drums picked up, and the strains of their most popular song filled the air, and Riley let Carl lead her into the shadows and off the stage.

"Did that just happen?" she asked.

Carl put his arm around her and said, "Welcome to the family, Riley."

She grinned and grinned, because she'd just gotten engaged to the Sexiest Man Alive. Her rockstar. Her everything.

Christmastime

Evan woke, and it took him a few seconds to remember he'd arrived on the island of Getaway Bay the night before. He'd wanted Riley to stay with him, but they weren't married yet, and she had a house of her own on the island. In fact, once they were married, whenever they came to Getaway Bay, they'd live in her house.

Carl had bought the one Evan had rented fifteen months ago, and he had himself a girlfriend to boot.

A loud knock on the door told Evan that Carl was awake, and then his brother entered. "You're getting married today."

Evan smiled as he stood up. "I sure am."

"And you're late already. Come on. Get in the shower. We have to be over to the resort in an hour."

"How long do you think it takes me to shower?"

"Think?" Carl asked. "Brother, I *know* how long it

takes you to get ready, and we're going to be late. Get in. Now."

"Maybe I've changed this year," Evan said.

Carl just laughed as he left Evan's bedroom, and Evan couldn't really argue. He had definitely changed in the last year, but that stemmed all the way back to when he'd walked into that coffee shop and seen that beautiful brunette.

Riley hadn't gone back to the dark locks, not that Evan minded. He loved her auburn hair, her freckles, everything about her. She'd been back in Hawaii for a month now, finishing the preparations for their big day. They'd stay on the island chain for a few days, celebrate Christmas with her family, and then he was taking her around the world for thirty days to see all the amazing cities she hadn't seen yet.

Osaka. Bangkok. Copenhagen. Berlin. London. Oslo. He hadn't been to all the places they were going, and he couldn't wait to experience them with his wife.

His *wife*.

He wanted to make new memories with that word and keep them with him for the rest of his life. So he let Carl retie his bow tie and drive them around the island to the patch of beach Riley could see from her back deck. His back deck soon enough.

Because Georgia Panic hadn't been touring this year, they'd spent plenty of time on the island of Getaway Bay together. He had joined the billionaire club, and it turned out that he liked Fisher and Jasper and Tyler and the other men and women. A lot. Sure, some were a bit stuffier than others, but for the most part, they were just people—like him.

The ocean breeze rippled the sides of the tent, but Riley had said she didn't care. She'd always envisioned herself getting married on the beach, even from childhood. As they'd talked and planned and visited various beaches, this one she'd had a bird's eye view of for so long had become the clear favorite. Plus, then they could see it every time they ate dinner on the back deck, a constant reminder of how much they loved each other.

She'd had sketches she'd done at some point in the past for the altar, the tent over it, the chairs, the colors. Evan had simply sat with her at the table while she showed everything to him. Then they'd gone to Your Tidal Forever, and she'd given everything to Lisa and Charlotte.

Charlotte was a bit of a handywoman, and she'd helped build the altar. Lisa had taken care of absolutely everything else. Riley had not allowed him to pay for anything except the rehearsal dinner and the honeymoon, claiming she'd been "saving forever" to get married.

Evan would've done anything for her. Gone to any lengths. Paid any amount. He just wanted the woman to be by his side for the rest of his life.

"Hurry up, Evan," Lisa said as soon as he opened the door. "Riley is going to be out in ten minutes, and you absolutely cannot see her in the dress before the wedding." She tugged on his arm, and Evan chuckled.

"We're not even late."

"Uh," Carl said at the same time Lisa said, "Yes, you are. Twenty minutes late."

"Oh, sorry," Evan said, shooting Carl a look. He just smiled and walked in the opposite direction. Evan watched him twine his fingers with his girlfriend's, and they went to sit by Evan's parents in the front row. Brett was there too, but he'd broken up with the woman he was dating and hadn't brought anyone to Getaway Bay for these nuptials.

Lisa ushered him into a tent that was barely big enough for him to hold out both arms. It was divided by another tent flap, and she gave him a very stern look, those blue eyes blazing with fire. "You do not go on the other side of this. Do you hear me?"

"Yes, ma'am," he said, because he'd do whatever she said when she barked at him like that.

She nodded and went out the way she'd come in. A few seconds later, he heard her voice on the other side of the divider, and he knew: Riley was over there. Maybe he could just peek....

"Nope," he muttered to himself. Not only did he not need Lisa's wrath on his wedding day, he wanted Riley to be happy. And she didn't want to see him yet. He paced from one end of the tent to the other, but it was only three steps for his long legs, and he was suddenly very glad he'd been twenty minutes late. Being cooped up here for a half an hour would've been torture.

The sound of fabric swishing met his ears, and he spun toward it. Lisa poked her head through. "I'm going to get her dad. I will come for you in two minutes."

"Thanks, Lisa," he said brightly.

She grinned and dropped the curtain. Evan immediately moved over to it and waited. Five seconds. Then ten. Satisfied that Lisa had left the tent on Riley's side, he said in a soft voice, "Riley?"

Her perfectly manicured fingers moved through the tiny gap in the curtain, and he seized onto them. "Almost time," she whispered.

"I love you," he said.

"I was worried you wouldn't show up," she said. "Twenty minutes late? Who arrives to their wedding with only ten minutes to spare?"

"Hey, my manager has the day off," he said. "And Carl wasn't rushing me. Did you really think I wouldn't show up?"

"No." She squeezed his fingers. "I can't wait to see you."

"I don't mind if you take a peek now," he said. "It's not my dress you can't see."

She giggled, and her hand slipped away from his to pull the curtain back hardly at all. He could see a sliver of her face, and she said, "Wow, you look great."

"I'm sure you do too."

"Riley," Lisa said, and Riley ducked away from the

curtain, her explanation that she hadn't been too close and he hadn't seen anything. Lisa's frustrated face filled the gap and she narrowed her eyes at Evan. "Did you see her dress?'

"I swear I didn't." Evan held up both hands in surrender. "I didn't touch that curtain."

"He didn't," Riley said from the other side. "Go on, now. I don't want this to start late. You know how I hate it when weddings start late."

Lisa grumbled something under her breath, but she yanked the curtain closed in the next moment. Evan waited for her to make the trek from doorway to doorway, and he apologized again when she arrived.

She was a master at hiding her emotions, because she said, "All right, Evan. Time to get you in place. Come with me, please." She led him out of the staging tent and toward the altar.

It was a beautiful piece of polished driftwood—at least that was what it looked like. The top had been sanded flat, and pink, white, and red flowers spilled off all the sides. He saw his parents smiling at him in the front row. His brothers. Riley's parents and her mob of a family. He'd met them all several times throughout the past year or so, and he couldn't help scooping up the toddler that ran toward him.

"Heya, Bri," he cooed to the little girl.

Her mother, Riley's sister, arrived a moment later. "Sorry, Evan."

"It's fine." He passed the girl back to Lauren. "No problem."

She turned and headed back to her seat, and Evan waved to his billionaire buddies, as well as Charlie and Amelia, and a few friends and neighbors he'd gotten to know.

His bandmates sat in the second and third row right behind his parents, and they all got up to give him hearty hugs. "Finally doing this," Dan said. "I can't believe it."

"Congrats," Hank said.

DJ just grabbed onto him and held him tight before returning to sit beside his girlfriend. They'd been dating for six years, and Evan had never asked him why they hadn't gotten married. Peter did the band handshake and hugged Evan, saying, "She's lucky to have you, man."

But Evan felt like the lucky one. Beyond lucky.

"Right here," Lisa said, positioning him in a little crook of the driftwood. "Don't move." She nodded to someone else, and then she went and took her seat with all of Riley's friends from Your Tidal Forever.

Evan had attended all of the rehearsals possible. He had been in LA the last few days, simply to assure his agent and record producer that yes, Georgia Panic had been writing songs all year. They had four new tracks already recorded, thank you very much, and were easily going to meet the deadlines set forth by TriCities.

Music filled the air, and Evan turned around, despite Lisa's warnings for him not to move. Riley stood at the end of the aisle now, her hand linked delicately in her father's. She was stunning, with a gorgeous lace design on the top part of her dress. Her skin glistened in the gaps of the lace on her arms and shoulders, but her bodice was covered. The dress fell down in straight layers from there, and though she walked under a gauzy tent, the sunshine still illuminated something sparkly on the fabric.

She wore her hair up in a sophisticated style, with perfect makeup, and that smile. Oh, that smile could undo all of Evan's defenses.

Pure joy filled him as their eyes locked. Her father whispered something to her and pressed a kiss to her cheek before passing her to Evan. "Bless you, my boy," he said before going to sit down.

The wedding party took their spots on either side of the altar, and one of Riley's brothers came around to the head of it. Jason smiled at both Riley and Evan before saying, "What a great day, right?"

Everyone cheered and laughed, and Evan's dreams of a non-stuffy wedding came true. Jason gave a little advice and talked about the sanctity of marriage for a couple of minutes. Then he said, "And you two have your own vows to read. Riles?"

She cleared her throat and accepted a slip of paper from Winnie, her niece. She didn't look at it, though, before she said, "Evan, I knew something magical was going to happen with you from the moment I laid eyes on you in that coffee shop. I didn't know what. I didn't even know who you were at the time. You never know what time it is, despite owning *several* watches."

Evan chuckled and ducked his head, because she was right.

"You need someone to give you your schedule every day. You can't cook." She smiled through everything she said, tears gathering in those lovely eyes. "But you can sing. And you are the best entertainer in the world. The sexiest man alive, in fact. And you love me perfectly, which is all that really matters to me."

Her voice broke, and Evan's eyes started to burn as tears rushed into them.

"I love you, and I will do my best to be your wife, your companion, your support." She handed the paper back to Winnie, and Evan's stomach seized.

"I didn't write anything down," he said, glancing around like a niece would bring him a slip of paper to read from.

She squeezed his hands, and he looked at her again, the lyrics to a new love song coming to his mind.

"I knew when I saw you in the coffee shop that I was going to try to leave with your number. I'd never been so happy to lose my watch." He drew in a deep breath. "You mean everything to me. You light the night for me. Make me feel alive. I don't want to do anything by myself anymore, because everything is better with you."

He took a microstep closer, almost leaning in to say, "I love you, and I will do my best to make sure you're happy for the rest of our lives together." He was glad he hadn't lost his composure, and they faced Jason again.

"Aw, you two are the cutest," he said, and Riley

giggled, though she'd told Evan she'd warned Jason against going off the script. "By the power vested in me by the state of Hawaii, I now pronounce you husband and wife." He grinned at them. "You may kiss your bride, rockstar."

Evan pulled Riley flush against him and leaned down. "I love you."

"Love you, too."

He kissed her to the best applause in the world—better than stadiums full of people, and music halls full of fans. Because these were their friends and family, and this was the beginning of the rest of their lives.

There's another bride coming to Getaway Bay! Read on to meet Lisa - a consultant at Your Tidal Forever - and carpenter Cal in **THE ISLAND STORM.**

Sneak Peek! The Island Storm
Chapter One

Lisa Ashford tucked her hair behind her ear and looked down at her to-do list. Nearly everything had been crossed off, as she'd been bustling around the office for the past several hours.

Only one item remained, and she'd been putting it off for a reason. But the company's spring barbecue sat only hours away now, and someone needed to approach Hope for the keys to the van so they could get all the food loaded up.

Shannon had organized the company party for a couple of years now, but this new spring barbecue had fallen to Lisa, as she had the fewest brides getting married this summer and fall. Organizing a barbecue played right to her strengths, and she hadn't minded calling around to find the perfect location—the private pool on the twenty-sixth floor at the Sweet Breeze Resort and Spa, thank you very much—ordering food, making invitations, and designing a theme.

In fact, all of that made Lisa's soul sing. But getting budget approvals from Hope had been the bane of her party planning, and the owner of Your Tidal Forever ruthlessly questioned everyone who wanted to use one of the company vans as if they'd be taking the ugly mom-vehicles on joyrides.

A flash of a smile touched Lisa's lips at the same time she wished she owned a mom-vehicle. Then she'd be a mother, something she wanted very badly. But her dating luck seemed to have run out years ago, despite everyone's reassurances that she'd find the perfect guy for her.

She'd tried the singles app that had matched a lot of people on the island of Getaway Bay in recent years, but she only found more guys looking for a good time or unwilling to commit. Or maybe they didn't like blondes. Whatever it was, she'd deleted her profile as a New Year's resolution, and she'd resorted to more traditional methods of finding a man.

Which meant she hadn't been out with anyone in four months. The only men she came in contact with were already married or about to be. Didn't leave her much room to get someone's number.

Steeling herself, she tugged down the hem of her blouse and clicked her way down the hall to Hope's office. The woman had been working less and less the past few months, and Lisa actually wondered if she was getting ready to sell the company. Maybe she was sick.

Something. Hope wasn't the same as she'd been, Lisa knew that.

Shannon already sat in her office, and Lisa was glad for the buffer. "Excuse me, Hope?" she asked. "We've got everything ready for the barbecue tonight, and I just need keys to the van to get things loaded up."

"Sure." Hope gave her a weary smile and opened one of her desk drawers. "Just one set?"

"Yes," she said as Shannon rose from her chair. She took the keys and handed them to Lisa as she joined her near the door.

"Have fun," Hope said, looking back down at her appointment book.

"Are you not coming?" Lisa asked, true surprise moving through her.

"I am," Hope said, glancing up again. "But I'll be a little late."

"Oh, okay." Lisa didn't know what else to say. She'd worked with Hope for a decade now, and she would've liked to have been better friends with her boss. But she wasn't, and she had the keys, so she turned and left the office.

Shannon came right on her heels, murmuring, "She and Aiden are having some problems."

Instant regret about her somewhat poisonous thoughts hit Lisa. "Oh, that's too bad." She paused at the door of Shannon's office. "You're still helping me with the setup, right?"

"Yes, let me put on my jeans and change my shoes."

Lisa wished she'd thought that far ahead. Hope liked everyone in the office to be dressed to the nines, and the dress code was actually something Lisa liked. She loved cute dresses and skirts, brightly colored tops, shoes with jewels on them, and jewelry. Oh, the jewelry. She probably owned a hundred bangles, and she was always looking for more.

Her shoes today were wedges, and she'd be fine carrying in napkins wearing shoes like that. They did have ribbons, which made her happy. And besides, she'd just stop at the front desk and ask for the bell service to bring out a cart to load everything on to.

Several minutes later, she and Shannon filled the van with cases of soda, paper products, and decorations. The Happy Hamburger was providing all of the food, and they'd have their own people deliver it only fifteen minutes before the party began.

"Ready?" she asked as Shannon tossed in the last package of paper plates.

"So ready," she said. "This spring has been brutal, hasn't it?"

"Only for you," Lisa said.

"Losing Riley has been hard," Shannon said as she started for the passenger door. Lisa got behind the wheel and buckled her seatbelt, a wail of missing for her best friend pulling through her. If she'd known Shannon was talking about how brutal things were personally, then yes, this spring without Riley had been terrible.

"I know," she said, because Riley had left Your Tidal

Forever four months ago. Left Lisa to deal with her bad dates on her own. Left the island in favor of working as the manager for her boyfriend's band.

Lisa didn't blame her; if she had a rich, celebrity boyfriend who'd offered her a dream job, she would've taken it too.

She just missed her best friend. She had other friends at the office, of course. But they had boyfriends or husbands, and Lisa felt like she was suffering in silence.

She navigated the traffic in East Bay, finally getting on the one road that went over to Getaway Bay, where the resort was. After pulling into the valet circle, she let Sterling open her door, giving him a bright smile.

"Heya, Sterling," she said.

"Miss Lisa," he said, the tips of his ears turning bright red. She half-liked his reaction to her, and half-disliked it. She didn't want to intimidate men, and he'd never asked her out. Maybe she should just ask him.

"We're going to need one of your fancy carts," she said, still toying with the idea of leaving this party with a date. "And Howie from The Happy Hamburger is bringing our food in forty-five minutes."

"I've got it on the schedule," he said. "I'll call Paul for you." He stepped over to his podium and picked up the phone while Shannon opened the back of the van.

Lisa thought about picking up a package of plastic forks—she could carry *something* upstairs—when a man said, "Evening, ladies. Need some help?"

"Wow, that was fast," Lisa said, turning. She expected to see someone from the resort there, a cart at the ready.

She found Cal Lewiston.

Tall, broad, bearded Cal Lewiston.

Her breath caught and her pulse skipped. "Hey," she said, her thoughts moving from Sterling to Cal. "What are you doing here?"

"There's a barbecue tonight, right?" He looked puzzled as he met her eyes and then let his gaze slide behind her to the van.

"Yeah, but not for another hour," Lisa said, appreciating his stature, all those muscles.... Why hadn't she thought of him as a possible date? He owned his own carpentry business on the island, but Your Tidal Forever did a ton of contract work with him.

"Oh, well, I guess I'm early." He grinned at her, and that so wasn't fair. Maybe Lisa's brain had been fried because of all this party prep. Maybe she just hadn't seen Cal for a while. Maybe she was just so incredibly lonely, or she hadn't been out with a man in so long, or something, that she couldn't seem to look away from the handsome lines of his face. That strong nose, that square jaw, those deep, dark blue eyes.

The hair on his head and face was a lighter brown, and he ran one hand along his jaw in what appeared to be a nervous tic.

"All of this?" another man asked, and Lisa jumped. The real bellhop had just arrived, and thankfully,

Shannon answered for her. She stepped out of the way as Cal and Paul started loading everything from the back of the van onto a cart, and then they all rode up to the twenty-sixth floor together.

A COUPLE OF HOURS LATER, LISA STOOD TO THE SIDE OF the soda table, her third diet cola in her hand. The barbecue had been going well enough. The food had arrived. Everyone from Your Tidal Forever had too—including Hope and her husband Aiden. He worked as a photographer for the company, and Lisa didn't detect any strain between them.

People were changing into their swimming suits, but Lisa hadn't brought one of those either. In the next moment, the music started, just as Owen, the general manager here at Sweet Breeze, had assured her it would. *Six o'clock, on the dot*, she thought, glad everything was running smoothly.

Everyone seemed to have someone they were talking to, especially since plus-ones had been encouraged for this company party. As the seconds ticked by, Lisa felt more and more like disappearing. She, of course, had not invited anyone to come with her. Sure, she had a cousin somewhere on the island, but it wasn't like she was besties with her.

Both of her sisters lived on Oahu, and one was

married and the other was probably on a hot date with her very serious boyfriend. She could call them, but they wouldn't be able to do anything. So Lisa was alone. Always alone.

Then her eyes caught on Cal.

He sat at a table by himself, a glass of bright pink lemonade in front of him. He hadn't brought a plus-one either. Without thinking, Lisa started toward him. With every step, her heartbeat pulsed faster and faster. What was she even going to say?

He lifted his drink to his lips and swallowed, the movement in his throat somehow making the temperature of Lisa's blood go up.

"Hey," she said when she arrived. The song switched to something slower, and she blurted the first thing that came to her mind. "Do you want to dance with me?"

Cal looked up, pure surprise in those gorgeous eyes. He didn't answer immediately, which only made Lisa more nervous. She reached for his drink and drained the last couple of swallows before setting it back on the table. "I promise not to step on your feet."

He tracked every movement, something playful sparking in his eyes. "All right," he said, standing up.

She wasn't sure if that was a good *all right* or a pity one. In this moment, it didn't matter. She wasn't going to stand on the sidelines during the social hour of this party. And she couldn't leave early.

"Great." She turned away from him, cursing herself

for this dance invitation. What if the man had a girlfriend? Surely he did, because a male specimen as good-looking as him didn't stay single for long. Maybe he just hadn't invited her to this party. Maybe she'd had to work. So many maybe's, and Lisa actually wanted to turn off her brain.

"Watch out," someone called. Maybe Cal. Maybe not.

Lisa flinched, not really sure what she was supposed to watch out for. A basketball hit her in the hip, and she felt her leg buckle.

A cry came from her throat as she tipped, and she only had enough time to realize what was happening before she toppled right into the swimming pool.

Shock coursed through her, though the water wasn't cold, and she came up sputtering. Her hair. Her makeup. Her dangly earrings.

Her clothes.

Lisa sucked at the air, pure humiliation filling her, and filling her, and filling her. It was fine. She'd just get out of the pool and dry off somewhere no one would find her.

"You okay?" a man asked, and Lisa just nodded, still trying to catch her breath and hide at the same time.

"I got you," Cal said, reaching down and hauling her out of the pool as if she weighed nothing. "After all, you owe me a dance."

Oh my heck! I can't wait to find out when Cal and Lisa have their first dance…

Read THE ISLAND STORM today!

Books in the Getaway Bay Romance series

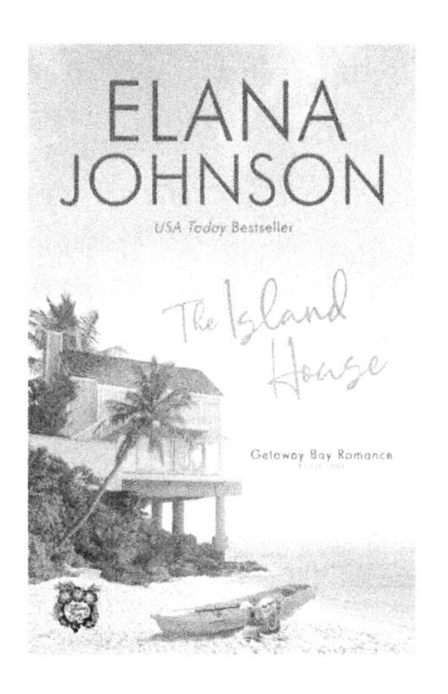

The Island House (Book 1): Charlotte Madsen's whole world came crashing down six months ago with the words, "I met someone else."

Can Charlotte navigate the healing process to find love again?

The Island Scandal (Book 2): Ashley Fox has known three things since age twelve: she was an excellent seamstress, what her wedding would look like, and that she'd never leave the island of Getaway Bay. Now, at age 35, she's been right about two of them, at least.

Can Burke and Ash find a way to navigate a romance when they've only ever been friends?

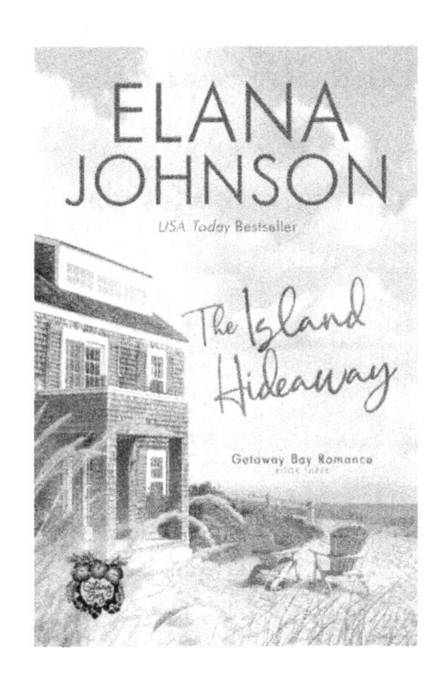

The Island Hideaway (Book 3): She's 37, single (except for the cat), and a synchronized swimmer looking to make some extra cash. Pathetic, right? She thinks so, and she's going to spend this summer housesitting a cliffside hideaway and coming up with a plan to turn her life around.

Can Noah and Zara fight their feelings for each other as easily as they trade jabs? Or will this summer shape up to be the one that provides the romance they've each always wanted?

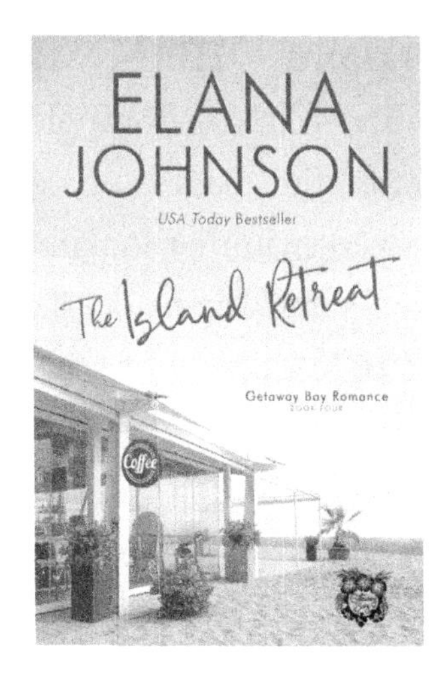

The Island Retreat (Book 4): Shannon's 35, divorced, and the highlight of her day is getting to the coffee shop before the morning rush. She tells herself that's fine, because she's got two cats and a past filled with emotional abuse. But she might be ready to heal so she can retreat into the arms of a man she's known for years...

The Island Escape (Book 5): Riley Randall has spent eight years smiling at new brides, being excited for her friends as they find Mr. Right, and dating by a strict set of rules that she never breaks. But she might have to consider bending those rules ever so slightly if she wants an escape from the island...

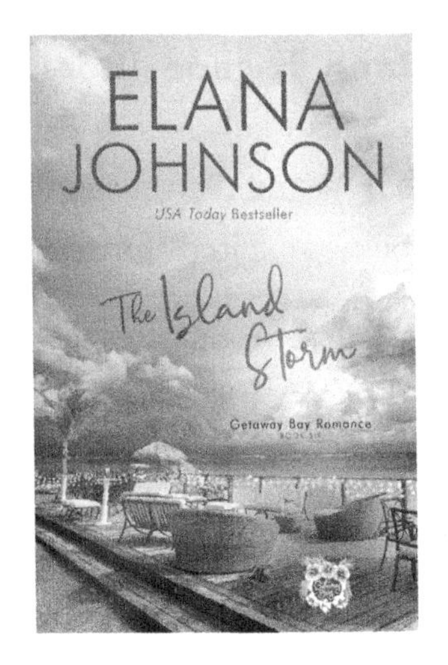

The Island Storm (Book 6): Lisa is 36, tired of the dating scene in Getaway Bay, and practically the only wedding planner at her company that hasn't found her own happy-ever-after. She's tried dating apps and blind dates...but could the company party put a man she's known for years into the spotlight?

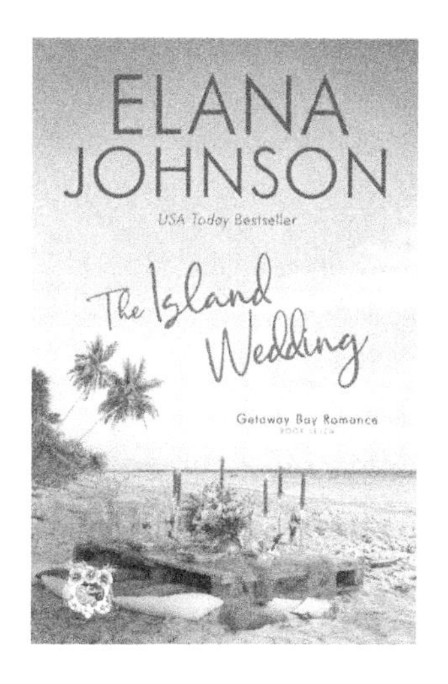

The Island Wedding (Book 7): Deirdre is almost 40, estranged from her teenaged daughter, and determined not to feel sorry for herself. She does the best she can with the cards life has dealt her and she's dreaming of another island wedding...but it certainly can't happen with the widowed Chief of Police.

Books in the Getaway Bay Resort Romance series

Aloha Hideaway Inn (Book 1): Can Stacey and the Aloha Hideaway Inn survive strange summer weather, the arrival of the new resort, *and* the start of a special relationship?

Getaway Bay (Book 2): Can Esther deal with dozens of business tasks, unhappy tourists, *and* the twists and turns in her new relationship?

Women's Beach Club (Book 3): With the help of her friends in the Beach Club, can Tawny solve the mystery, stay safe, and keep her man?

Straw and Diamonds (Book 4): Can Sasha maintain her sanity amidst their busy schedules, her issues with men like Jasper, and her desires to take her business to the next level?

The Billionaire Club (Book 5): Can Lexie keep her business affairs in the shadows while she brings her relationship out of them? Or will she have to confess everything to her new friends...and Jason?

Sweet Breeze Resort (Book 6): Can Gina manage her business across the sea and finish the remodel at Sweet Breeze, all while developing a meaningful relationship with Owen and his sons?

Rainforest Retreat (Book 7): As their paths continue to cross and Lawrence and Maizee spend more and more time together, will he find in her a retreat from all the family pressure? Can Maizee manage her relationship with her boss, or will she once again put her heart—and her job—on the line?

Getaway Bay Singles (Book 8): Can Katie bring him into her life, her daughter's life, and manage her business while he manages the app? Or will everything fall apart for a second time?

Books in the Stranded in Getaway Bay Romance series

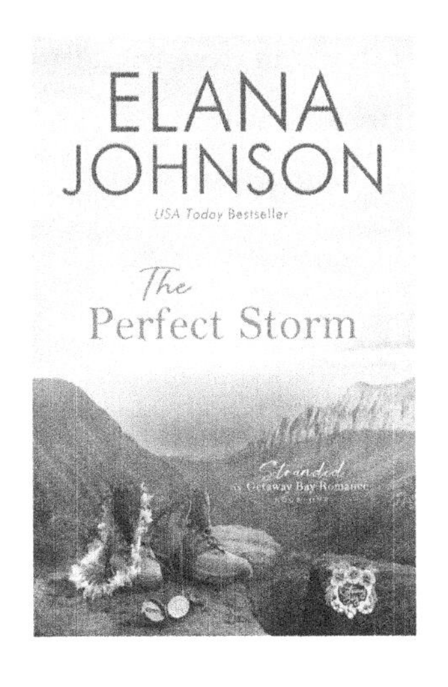

Love and Landslides (Book 1): A freak storm has her sliding down the mountain...right into the arms of her ex. As Eden and Holden spend time out in the wilds of Hawaii trying to survive, their old flame is rekindled. But with secrets and old feelings in the way, **will Holden be able to take all the broken pieces of his life and put them back together in a way that makes sense? Or will he lose his heart and the reputation of his company because of a single landslide?**

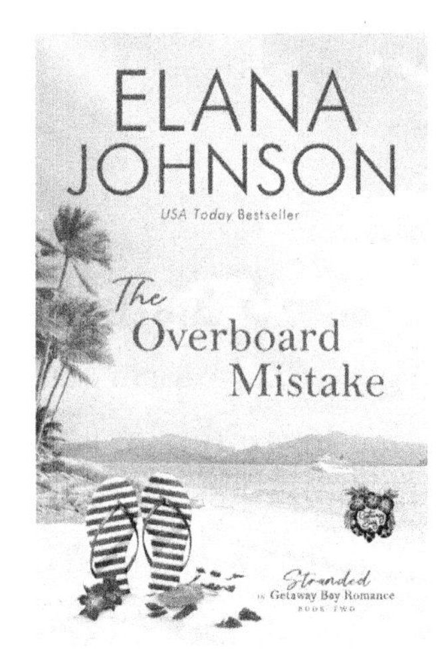

The Overboard Mistake (Book 2): Friends who ditch her. A pod of killer whales. A limping cruise ship. All reasons Iris finds herself stranded on an deserted island with the handsome Navy SEAL...

The Cruising Fiasco (Book 3): He can throw a precision pass, but he's dead in the water in matters of the heart...

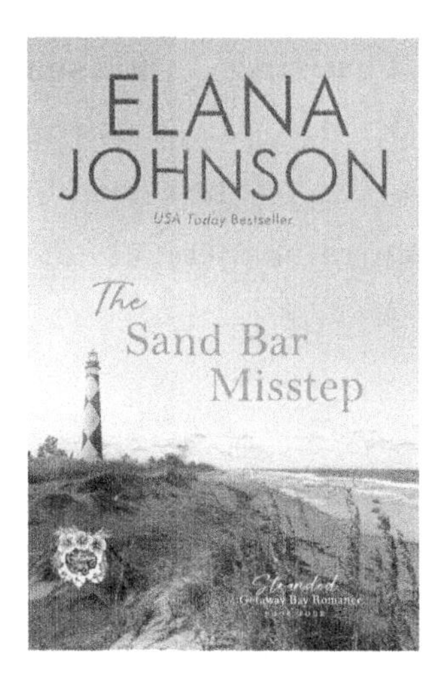

The Sand Bar Misstep (Book 4): Tired of the dating scene, a cowboy billionaire puts up an Internet ad to find a woman to come out to a deserted island with him to see if they can make a love connection...

About Elana

Elana Johnson is the USA Today bestselling author of dozens of clean and wholesome contemporary romance novels. She lives in Utah, where she mothers two fur babies, works full-time with her husband, and eats a lot of veggies while writing. Find her on her website at elanajohnson.com.

Made in the USA
Monee, IL
09 June 2022

97753996R00152